A House of Mysteries

A Shade of Vampire, Book 43

Bella Forrest

Also by Bella Forrest:

THE SECRET OF SPELLSHADOW MANOR

The Secret of Spellshadow
Manor (Book 1)
The Breaker (Book 2)

THE GENDER GAME

The Gender Game (Book 1)
The Gender Secret (Book 2)
The Gender Lie (Book 3)
The Gender War (Book 4)
The Gender Fall (Book 5)
The Gender Plan (Book 6)

A SHADE OF VAMPIRE SERIES:

Series 1:
Derek & Sofia's story:

A Shade of Vampire (Book 1)
A Shade of Blood (Book 2)
A Castle of Sand (Book 3)
A Shadow of Light (Book 4)
A Blaze of Sun (Book 5)
A Gate of Night (Book 6)
A Break of Day (Book 7)

Series 2:
Rose & Caleb's story:

A Shade of Novak (Book 8)
A Bond of Blood (Book 9)
A Spell of Time (Book 10)
A Chase of Prey (Book 11)
A Shade of Doubt (Book 12)
A Turn of Tides (Book 13)
A Dawn of Strength (Book 14)
A Fall of Secrets (Book 15)
An End of Night (Book 16)

Series 3: The Shade continues with a new hero…

A Wind of Change (Book 17)
A Trail of Echoes (Book 18)
A Soldier of Shadows (Book 19)
A Hero of Realms (Book 20)
A Vial of Life (Book 21)
A Fork Of Paths (Book 22)
A Flight of Souls (Book 23)
A Bridge of Stars (Book 24)

Series 4:
A Clan of Novaks

A Clan of Novaks (Book 25)
A World of New (Book 26)
A Web of Lies (Book 27)
A Touch of Truth (Book 28)

For an updated list of Bella's books, please visit her website:
www.bellaforrest.net

Join Bella's VIP email list and she'll personally send you an email
reminder as soon as her next book is out! Visit here to sign up:
www.forrestbooks.com

Contents

New Generation List

- **Aida:** daughter of Bastien and Victoria (half werewolf/half human)
- **Field:** biological son of River, adopted son of Benjamin (mix of Hawk and vampire-half-blood)
- **Jovi:** son of Bastien and Victoria (half werewolf/half human)
- **Phoenix:** son of Hazel and Tejus (sentry)
- **Serena:** daughter of Hazel and Tejus (sentry)
- **Vita:** daughter of Grace and Lawrence (part-fae/human)

SERENA
[HAZEL AND TEJUS'S DAUGHTER]

My vision was blurring, my breath coming out in short, tight rasps.

I'm having a panic attack.

I kept my head between my knees, trying to regulate my breathing as best I could. It was dark, but the greenhouse behind me showered the long grass of the lawn in a soft glow. I kept my eyes fixed on a single point—one grass stem, a little taller than the others, that I could use to anchor myself.

I don't want to lose control.

I wouldn't, and *couldn't*, fall apart. I had friends and family relying on me to stay strong. That was really the cornerstone law of GASP—you never gave up. No matter what the circumstances, or how dark and lonely and hopeless it all felt, you kept going.

No matter if it felt like the world as you knew it was crumbling around you.

I took another deep breath, and felt steady enough to raise my head and look around at the wild, unkempt garden that surrounded me. Most of it was in shadow, the only light coming from the pale moonlight and the windows of the old plantation house that were lit by the yellow kerosene lamps. I didn't like being out here on my own—not after my last night-time experience in the swamps, which lay just outside the boundaries of the garden up ahead. I averted my eyes, reminding myself that Field was somewhere up on the roof or settled in one of the large trees that grew up around the building. Wherever he was, it wouldn't be far—we had been told not to leave the grounds, and it was the one instruction from the Druid that we were finally willing to obey.

I leaned back against the glass of the greenhouse, listening to the mating call of the crickets and the silence that came from the swamps and jungle beyond. It was an unnatural silence—as if out there, in the darkness, creatures held their breath. Anticipating, perhaps, that I'd be stupid enough to venture out there again.

Not going to happen, I silently informed the darkness.

The security of the house might have been a double-edged sword, in that we were technically safe from the creatures that populated the rest of Eritopia—the shape-shifters and the Destroyers we had come across so far—but the security of the house didn't feel comforting when it seemed that we were trapped there, with no way out and no hope of our families coming to get us. The latter was something that my friends and brother weren't yet aware of. It would fall on me to pass on the news—another crushing blow to add to our current situation.

Trying to delay the conversation, if only for a few more moments so that I could get my own head around the news before passing it on, I looked up at the blanket of stars which shone in the pitch-black sky. When I was in The Shade, looking up at the stars had always been reassuring, exciting even, knowing that there was this great, wide world on the doorstep in which I was nothing but a small speck. It gave me a sense of freedom, of huge possibility to do or be whatever I wanted. Now it just made me afraid. I didn't recognize any of the shapes or patterns here, not like I did back home.

I'd never been knowledgeable about astronomy—not like Vita was—but I'd shown interest enough to come up with my own dumb names for constellations and keep my fingers crossed for shooting stars at certain times of the year. The sky above me was completely unfamiliar. Eritopia, a set of stars that included the land we were currently inhabiting, was deep in the void of the In-Between. The only place I would recognize in this dimension was the four stars of the fae, but I couldn't see them in the night sky, and considering how vast the In-Between was reported to be by Corrine and the other members of GASP, I could only conclude we were a long, long way from where we were meant to be.

Knowing that I shouldn't delay the inevitable any longer, I scanned the surrounding trees for Field. Not seeing him, I sighed and reluctantly walked back into the damp warmth of the greenhouse. I'd call him from the window once I got upstairs—it was probably best to tell everyone at the same time. Like ripping off a Band-Aid in one go.

I didn't see or hear any sign of the Druid. I had left him

back in his strange laboratory—a room covered in strange jars and beakers, full of unknown and dubious-looking substances. And the flame. The flame that had somehow shown me everything I'd never wanted to see.

Not wanting to spend time alone in the downstairs part of the house, which I considered the Druid's domain, I headed straight for the staircase. We had taken over the second floor, sharing rooms like we were in a boarding-school dormitory, ensuring that we remained together—as if that would somehow keep the strangeness of the place at bay.

Once I reached the hallway, I headed for the last room on the left, where Vita and Aida would be sleeping. Wishing I didn't need to disturb them from much-needed sleep, I pushed the door open, surprised to see another lamp glowing in the room and both Vita and Aida sitting upright on the bed.

"Why are you up?" I asked, before noticing their pale, horrified expressions. Clearly something had happened while I'd been gone. I scanned the room, trying to gauge the danger. I could see nothing unusual—well, nothing other than the same dilapidated, shabby room that looked like a movie set for a historical drama, completely at odds with the modern-day nightwear of my friends.

"I saw something," Vita whispered. "In the mirror…"

Her hands had started to shake, and she held them tightly together in her lap. Whatever she had seen had obviously terrified the life out of her. Aida placed her hands over Vita's, trying to provide a wordless comfort that our friend so clearly needed.

"Vita?" I pressed. She wasn't the most forthcoming person, even under normal circumstances. I wondered if I should just hear the story from Aida, but when I turned to her, Aida's golden eyes were as troubled and confused as I imagined mine were.

Changing tack, I sat down on the bed. My news could wait until Vita shared her burden. It wasn't like we could do anything about the circumstances we were in anyway—there was no action to be taken, only acceptance of the fact that we were in far deeper trouble than we'd previously imagined.

"I'm sorry," Vita replied, shaking her head as if to remove some mental image she didn't want lodged there. "It was terrifying. I just…God, I *hate* this place."

I knew exactly how she felt. Would there be any moment here when we wouldn't all be terrified out of our minds?

For both Vita and Aida, it was worse. I was afraid for *them*, and what might lurk outside of our safe-house…they were afraid of what they might *become*, what was happening to their bodies and minds as they transformed into all-seeing Oracles—a 'gift' (in the loosest possible definition of the word) left to them by the Oracle our parents had discovered living in Nevertide almost two decades ago.

"Just tell us what happened," I replied gently. "We need to know. We can help." Vita looked over at me with a look of disbelief mirrored in her turquoise eyes.

Yeah, okay. Overstatement.

We probably couldn't help at all, but that wasn't the point. Whatever Vita had just seen in the mirror, she needed to share it.

She nodded, and started to tell us what had happened, her voice high and tight, as if she only half-believed what she was saying.

"I was in the shower, because I was too hot and couldn't sleep. When I got out, I looked in the mirror. Then my face—it started to change, to *distort*. I thought it was me. I was tired…but then the face definitely became someone else. It was a woman, with pale blue eyes and white hair. She called out my name, asking me if I was there—if I could hear her. I couldn't reply. I just froze… I wanted to say something, she sounded so desperate to speak to me. Then she vanished, and I called out, but she'd gone."

"Was it a vision?" I asked. So far, Vita was the only one who had been experiencing the 'gift'—I thought that was maybe because of her latent fae genes, that somehow they made her more attuned to the change, but I wasn't sure.

Vita shook her head.

"I don't think so… it was different. I didn't feel the nausea, and it wasn't images in my mind—it was real. I promise you it was real."

"I don't doubt that," I hastened to reassure her. I almost wanted it to be a vision because the alternative was another layer of weirdness on our already totally bizarre circumstances.

"The woman sounds familiar," Aida replied slowly. "From the description—"

"I know," Vita agreed. "It sounds like the Nevertide Oracle was trying to make contact."

We all looked at one another, falling silent. It seemed we were all trying to work out whether this was good news, or bad. I guessed only time would tell.

Vita
[GRACE AND LAWRENCE'S DAUGHTER]

"We need to fetch the others," Serena said eventually. "I have some news of my own—it's not good."

"Did you manage to mind-meld with the Druid?" Aida asked, reminding me of Serena's mission tonight. She had waited till we thought the Druid would be asleep, planning to syphon off him while he was unprotected and hopefully unaware of what was happening to him.

Serena shook her head. "No. It didn't go as planned. He woke up—he's too on guard. But then he showed me something… I'll tell you everything when we're all here. I'll get the boys."

Serena stood up, moving toward the doorway. She had changed into a nightgown that she'd found in the closet— a white, frilly thing that would have looked ridiculous on anyone else, but managed to make Serena, with her poker-straight black hair that fell like a waterfall around her shoulders and her large blue eyes, look like a romantic heroine, about to be swept off her feet by some dashing highway robber or something.

I nodded gratefully at her suggestion. Having all of us together would make me feel a whole lot better, reminding me that I wasn't alone in this. Even if, so far, it had just been me seeing visions and getting accosted in the bathroom by the Oracle, a whole team of us would deal with it—deal with anything that this stupid house chose to throw our way.

When Serena had gone, Aida turned to me.

"When you said she sounded desperate, what did you mean?" she asked. "Like she was in trouble, or we were?"

It was a good question. One I wasn't sure I knew the answer to, not yet. I tried to recall everything just as it had happened, to move away from the shock and fear that her presence had brought up in me and remember the details.

"She just sounded frantic. And at the end, it was almost like something happened to cut her off—that her disappearance was against her will, not just because I hadn't answered."

Aida's expression grew even more concerned. I knew what she was thinking. The Druid had told us that the Oracle was in the custody of Azazel—already that name struck fear in me, and I hadn't come face-to-face with him yet. I didn't even know enough that I could say for sure that what the Druid had told us was true. Azazel was the ruler of Eritopia. He owned and controlled the repugnant Destroyers that had killed one of the incubi while we were in the jungle, Bijarki only just narrowly escaping the same fate. If the Oracle had tried to contact us without Azazel's permission, and been caught, she would be in danger. And so would we.

Before I could say anything more, the footsteps of the others came from the corridor. In the room next door, I heard a light thump, as if someone had dropped down onto the dusty floorboards. It must have been Field, coming in from the outside. Soon they were all gathered in our bedroom—Jovi looking sleep-rumpled with his black hair sticking up at odd angles. Phoenix and Field both stood leaning against the wall, Phoenix frowning with concern and Field looking wary, his eyes darting to the open windows as if he expected something to come flying through them at any moment. We were all on high alert.

Serena, never really able to sit still at the best of times, paced slowly up and down the room, chewing on her lip with worry.

"Vita," she said, coming to a standstill, "you'd better start."

With reluctance, I repeated the story again. I tried not to feel like a freak when the boys raised their eyebrows in surprise, staring at me as if they didn't recognize me anymore. I knew it was most likely my imagination—especially when the surprise gave way to a deep concern.

"Are you okay?" Field asked, when I'd finished explaining my theory that it was the Oracle who was trying to reach out to us.

"Just shaken," I replied evenly, not wanting anyone other than Serena and Aida to know how terrifying I'd found the whole thing. "And I want to know why she's trying to reach out to us—and whether or not we speak to the Druid about it."

Field shook his head.

"Not yet," he replied. "I think we keep this to ourselves. Until we know what message she's trying to pass on, I think it's better if the Druid doesn't know about it. Especially as she might be trying to help get us out of here."

"I agree," Phoenix added. "We don't know how much we can trust him—if at all."

"There's more," Serena added, resuming her pacing. "When I went downstairs to try to syphon off him, he woke and took me through to a laboratory he has—it's behind a hidden door in the basement room." I shuddered, thinking of the old-fashioned hospital beds that Phoenix, Aida and I had lain on while we were going through the transformation into Oracles. When we'd woken, I had thought for one crazy, horrible moment that we were in some kind of psych ward. I wasn't a fan of the basement, even if it was the coolest room in the baking-hot house.

"There's a flame in the room," she continued, "it's obviously some kind of magic—it rises from some rocks on the floor, but there's no fuel or anything to burn. Anyway, he told me to look inside the flame, and I saw our families in the In-Between, leaving the fire star to return home. None of them…" She hesitated, turning her back to us as she walked the other way. "None of them know we're missing. It's almost like we never existed in the first place."

"What?" Phoenix replied, his brow furrowing more deeply.

I waited for Serena to clarify what she meant. So far, none of what she'd said made any kind of sense to me. She began to repeat the conversations she'd heard between our parents. When she mentioned my mom and dad, I felt my body grow cold—as if the life was being sucked out of my veins.

"What did the Druid say?" Aida asked.

"He said the whole Eritopia region is surrounded by mists, like a force-field. As soon as someone passes into them, they cease to exist anywhere else. It's a way of protecting the area...making sure no one discovers it. I guess it stops people—other creatures from the In-Between—going back, or others following them."

"You believe him?" Jovi asked, echoing my own thoughts.

Serena shook her head. "That I don't know. It could all be a trick...but why bother? The only motive I can see for him lying to us is that we might give up hope GASP would come and rescue us, but it seems to be an extravagant way of accomplishing that, especially when things are feeling pretty hopeless anyway," Serena replied despondently. "And I'm starting to believe he's telling the truth—maybe not about everything, but some things at least."

"What makes you say that?" I asked. Serena was naturally skeptical—she questioned everything, and rarely took things on say-so alone. If someone declared something was a fact, she would want evidence—she would want to prove it, beyond all reasonable doubt. Serena wanted to study journalism, but I often wondered if she wouldn't be better off becoming some hotshot lawyer.

"A diary I found," she replied, looking sheepish. "I didn't mention it earlier, but it's something I found in one of the other rooms. It belonged to a woman who lived in this house, a long time ago—and I think she was an Oracle too. The Druid mentioned another Oracle was here before the Nevertide one, and she's the reason I don't think the Druid's making this all up. Her diary mentions the dangers outside—how the Druid's father was keeping her safe."

"And you didn't share this because?" Phoenix questioned his sister, his face darkening.

"Because I wanted to find something in it that would be genuinely useful," Serena replied. "I'm sorry I kept it quiet…I don't know." She shrugged. "I felt a weird bond with the woman. It was so personal, everything she'd written."

"Diaries *are* personal," Phoenix replied dryly. "We need to have a look at it."

Serena nodded, leaving the room without making eye contact with the rest of us.

"I just don't believe this," Jovi muttered. "How can we simply vanish from our parents' lives? From our own lives? I mean—what about all our *stuff*? The photographs around our houses? Does that all vanish too?"

No one could answer him. Any other questions we had would have to be put to the Druid when morning came. Then we'd just have to decide whether or not we were going to believe the answers he gave us.

Serena came back into the room, holding a small, leather-bound book. Its pages were clearly yellowed with age, as if the whole thing might crumble to ashes if a sudden gust of wind dashed through the window.

"It was written in the eighteen hundreds. Her name's Elissa." Serena opened the diary for us all to see. The handwriting was feminine, but cramped. On each page, I could almost sense the urgency with which she wrote everything down, the letters spiked, with ink blots here and there, indicating a sense of intensity—from rage, passion or frustration I didn't know.

"How can she write everything down if she's an Oracle?" Aida asked the obvious question. "I thought they were supposed to be blind?"

"I wondered that too," Serena agreed, her cheeks becoming flushed with excitement as she turned through the delicate pages. "But she never mentions it—and goes into detail about the house, the Druid's father…everything."

Serena fell silent.

"You should keep reading it," Field told her. "Find out what you can, especially anything about the side effects of visions, things like blindness or the lack of reproductive organs—the Oracle twins were barren, and blind. If this Oracle has found a way to circumvent that, I want us to know how."

Serena nodded, and Field turned to us all, his face thoughtful.

"I know tonight's been tough," he said, as Aida rolled her eyes. It was a huge understatement, and Field half-smiled. "It doesn't change anything, though. We still need to stick to our plan—using the Druid to help develop your Oracle abilities. Clearly, if the Druid is to be believed, using the visions is going to be our only chance of getting out of here."

I nodded. Field was right—our original plan wouldn't change. We would use the Druid for training purposes, getting him to help us develop the visions until we could use them for our own benefit. I didn't really know if I felt bad about our manipulation. If the Druid *was* on our side, as he claimed, then if we could find a way to get home safely and escape the clutches of Azazel, he would support us. If not, well—that would just be tough luck on his part. We weren't his puppets, and we never would be.

I looked around at the faces I knew so well—all of us in half shadow from the yellowing light of the lamp. Serena looked downcast and worried, her glance flicking to the diary she'd placed on the night stand as if she wanted all its answers, instantly. Jovi was almost motionless, clearly still in shock and trying to process the information we'd all shared in the last few hours. Aida was the same, her eyes practically burning a hole in the wall opposite as she stared unblinking at its mildewed surface. Phoenix just looked angry, and fierce—as if he was ready to battle our way out of the house and Eritopia, stopping at nothing to get us all home.

I agreed with Field, but I wasn't looking forward to what was to come. The vision I had experienced in the jungle had been horrible. Not just because of what I had seen, but the side-effects that had come with it. The gut-wrenching nausea, the weakness afterward—and the strange, disassociated state I'd found myself in, almost like I was half going insane. Would it always be like that? Was that what all Oracles endured when they had visions? I couldn't remember my parents or any other members of GASP mentioning what Oracles might experience…most probably because they had no clue. Oracles were rare things. Maybe it was something we'd just have to endure.

"You all need to get some rest," Field continued. "I know the visions have been rough on you, Vita—we'll speak to the Druid about that. See if there's anything he can do to help."

"Thanks," I replied, relieved that I wouldn't have to bring it up myself. I didn't exactly relish the thought of any more contact with the Druid than absolutely necessary. Out of all of us, Serena seemed to be the most accepting of him, but I supposed that was due to the fact he'd saved her life in the jungle. I guessed she had already decided he was the lesser of two evils.

Jovi rose off the bed, joining Phoenix and Field as they headed for the bedroom door.

"Yell if you need us," he replied, trying to smile.

As they left, Serena moved to pick up the diary, but Aida shot her a glance.

"Not tonight," Aida asserted. "We all need to sleep. You as well, Serena."

"Okay," she grumbled, her fingers flitting over its surface. I hoped for her sake the diary held some of the answers we were looking for. I got the impression it represented a life-raft for her, something to hold on to— something that might provide a thread of comfort. I wished I had something similar. As Aida put out the lamp, and we all lay on top of the musty sheets, I suddenly felt incredibly lonely, wondering how that could possibly be, with my two best friends lying on either side of me.

SERENA
[HAZEL AND TEJUS'S DAUGHTER]

The next morning, after finally getting some actual sleep, I had a shower and got dressed, planning to make my way down to breakfast early. I could practically smell the coffee from here. Vita and Aida were still sleeping, both of them pushing the other occasionally as they struggled for space on the bed. The four-poster was large enough for two, but my friends—Aida especially—moved a lot in her sleep, and we would need better sleeping arrangements going forward. I considered asking Phoenix to help me move one of the spare beds into our room, or moving to a different room entirely that would be large enough for all three of us, as I didn't really like the thought of being separated from them—especially if Vita continued to have night-time visits from the Nevertide Oracle.

Outside it was another blazing hot day. The sun had only just risen and already the heat was fast becoming intolerable. The ice-cold shower had done enough to wake me up, but already the sticky heat was taking over—it wouldn't be long before I was feeling drowsy and foggy again. Out in the distance a cloying mist had settled over the tops of the jungle and mountains, and I wondered if we might be due a tropical storm later.

Leaving the room and following the mouth-watering scent of fresh coffee, I made my way downstairs and into the dining room. I was surprised to see Field, Jovi and my brother already seated at the table.

"You're up early," I remarked, heading straight toward the pot of coffee before even bothering to take a seat. I poured it into a cup and instantly took a sip, not minding the liquid scalding the back of my throat.

"Too hot to sleep," Field replied in a thick voice, holding out his cup for me to fill.

"Have you seen the Druid yet?" I asked them.

Jovi shook his head.

"I was first down but I haven't seen him. Are the others awake?"

"Not yet," I replied, taking my seat and removing the plate warmers to reveal—surprise, surprise—the same oat pancakes as yesterday. I recalled Elissa's diary entries about the food—how quickly she gotten sick of eating the same thing day after day. For the time being, I was just glad we had food, but I didn't doubt that it wouldn't be long before I got sick of the monotony.

"Can you actually explain this?" Phoenix asked me, gesturing to the food and the coffee.

"I can sort of explain it," I replied. "The Druid hinted it was some beings called the 'Daughters of Eritopia' who put the house on a sort of magical loop." I furrowed my brow, trying to recall if he'd said anything else—the concept of the 'loop' didn't really make much sense to me. If the food was fresh every time we ate, why wasn't the house in better condition? Why was it so aged and crumbling?

"So we're going to be eating this every morning?" Jovi asked. "The same thing—every day?"

I nodded slowly, knowing how much food meant to Jovi. His werewolf genes meant that he needed to eat a lot, and frequently. It was the same with Aida. This diet was going to be difficult to maintain for them both…I was just glad for once that they weren't full werewolf. There would be no way they'd have enough energy for the change on this amount of food.

"Wow," he breathed. "Just for the record—*really* not liking this place."

"Did he say anything more about the Daughters?" Field asked, turning to me.

"Nothing more than we've already heard," I replied.

Field nodded, but my brother looked at me with a strange expression.

"You haven't been spending time with him, have you?" he asked, brow furrowing.

"No!" My reply was a little louder than intended. I put my cup down, and replied in a calmer manner, "No, I haven't. It was just during the time when you were out of it, and I was trying to find out as much information as I could. It's not like I've been deliberately seeking out his company."

Though my answer was perfectly honest, I could feel heat rising in my cheeks. Especially as Jovi had turned to stare at me, sharing the same quizzical expression as my brother.

This was getting awkward.

"We should speak to him more about the Daughters though," I continued, turning back to Field, who was the only one who didn't seem suspicious of the information I'd managed to gather so far—which, in truth, wasn't a lot. I couldn't understand why Phoenix was making a big deal of it—surely it was better to know this stuff, by whatever means necessary? Plus, Jovi and Field had encouraged me to find out information from the Druid—I was only doing what had been asked of me, for the benefit of us all.

"I agree. They obviously have a lot of power—they must, to accomplish something like this. As the guardians of Eritopia, they might have a way that we can get home, and perhaps reverse the effect of the mists..." Field trailed off, deep in thought.

"Do you think there will be a way we can contact them?" I asked eagerly.

"I have no idea. Which is why we will need to speak to the Druid."

"Or Bijarki," added Jovi. "He seems a bit more willing to talk to us than the Druid does."

It was true. The incubus, whatever reservations I had about him, did seem more open than the Druid had been so far. We would probably need to get him alone though—from the conversation we'd overheard the two of them having yesterday, it was clear that the Druid was the one in charge, the one masterminding whatever plan they were trying to set in motion. It would also help to know more about his kind—and, more importantly, why they had defected to Azazel's rule.

I reminded myself that I needed to have a word with Vita about the incubus. After the Druid's warning to him to stay away from the 'females', I had promised myself that I would warn her. It wasn't that I felt she was easy prey for him—I had just noticed that his charm tended to be directed toward her, and his gaze, whenever it lighted on her, intensified just enough to be noticeable. The conversation would need to be held in private though—she'd get embarrassed if I brought it up in front of the others.

"Morning." Aida greeted us with a sleepy smile as she and Vita entered the room. I made myself busy pouring them coffee, wondering when the Druid would also make an appearance.

Both Aida and Vita were still wearing their pajamas, and I made a mental note that clothing was another subject to discuss with the Druid. The boys were all still in their formal wear from the night of Sherus and Nuriya's party, their shirts now looking a lot worse for wear, and their pants filthy and ripped. We certainly looked like an odd bunch.

"How are you feeling?" I asked Vita after she'd taken a sip of coffee, and began nibbling at the oat pancakes.

"Better. Needed the sleep," she replied with a smile. Privately I felt she needed a lot more of it—there were purple shadows under her eyes, and she looked just as pale as she had been last night.

"Did anyone else have weird dreams?" Aida asked the table.

I looked at her in surprise. "No—what happened?"

She shrugged. "I can't even remember… They were vivid though—and I know that all of you were in them, just not what we were doing."

"Was it a nightmare?" Vita asked.

"No, I don't think so." Aida shook her head, looking puzzled as she tried to recall them. "Just weird."

"This might sound stupid, but maybe you should start keeping a dream journal or something?" I replied. "I read somewhere that it helps you remember your dreams…Now that you're an Oracle, maybe you should take them more seriously, try to keep track of them."

"It doesn't sound stupid," Field agreed. "They might be visions—or partial visions, getting mixed up with your subconscious. It's worth trying."

I smiled to myself. Now that Field had agreed with my suggestion, I could practically see Aida becoming a lot more receptive to something that she would have dismissed as hokey if only Vita or I had mentioned it. Aida caught my smile, and nudged me sharply under the table.

I turned toward the wall, hiding a snicker.

"Where's the Druid?" Aida asked loudly.

"We haven't seen him yet," Phoenix replied, leaning back in his chair. Almost as soon as the statement left my brother's lips, the Druid entered the room. He glanced over the remains of our breakfast, looking pleased that we'd managed to finish most of it. Mainly thanks to Jovi.

"Are you ready to begin training?" the Druid asked.

Phoenix glanced over at Vita and Aida. They both nodded.

"Okay," my brother replied, turning back to the Druid. "Where do we start?"

"By following me back to the basement."

Oh, great.

More time in the serial killer hangout. I wasn't sure what

was worse—the cold, damp rooms below the house, or the humid and blazing heat above it. Still, there was no way I'd miss out on the training session. I might have trusted the Druid more than the others, but I still wanted to keep an eye on him and my friends. I also had the feeling that this was something I wouldn't want to miss. It wasn't every day that your best friends and brother got to see into the future.

VitA
[GRACE AND LAWRENCE'S DAUGHTER]

We followed the Druid from the dining room, walking down the better-lit hallway till we came to the room where the Druid habitually sat in front of a roaring fire. To my astonishment, it was lit again, creating a sweltering room that was completely unnecessary considering the weather outside. Bijarki was standing by one of the windows, and he smiled broadly when he saw us, his gaze homing in on me and making me feel instantly uncomfortable. Well, more uncomfortable than I was feeling already. I was dreading the training session—the nausea of the visions, and the weakness I experienced after, but not only that. I was half worried I'd fail completely. That it would be like my fae abilities all over again, knowing that the power was in there somewhere, but not being able to access it properly. It would be humiliating, and there would be no Zerus to put my mind at ease.

I ignored Bijarki as best I could, and stepped in line next to Serena, shielding myself from his approach as we all descended the staircase to the basement.

It was cooler down here, and I was grateful for that, but it was also damp, and the smell was even more musty than in the rest of the house. The hospital beds were gone, which was a relief, but in their place were three metal tubs—dented and worn with age, and filled with water and ice.

"What are these?" exclaimed Serena the moment she entered the room. "They look like some kind of psychiatric torture. Tell me it's not for them?"

The Druid, with a slight but perceptible tightening of his jaw, ignored Serena and turned to the three of us—me, Aida and Phoenix. He cleared his throat, and began his lesson.

"The best way to bring about your visions is to get you into a semi-conscious state. The mind has a better chance of accessing itself if it's not trying to attend to the rest of your body—freeing it up, in a way. Ideally, we want your bodies in 'sleep' mode, while your brain is still active."

From the conversation we'd just been having about Aida's dreams, this made a lot of sense to me. I had also seen the Oracle when I was in a sort of semi-conscious state—my body bone tired, but my mind whirring with the events of the last few hours.

"We're going to replicate that state, using these." The Druid gestured to the ice baths. "The water will shock your body into slowing down the heart rate and metabolic process. Your brain will survive, going into overdrive while the body is neglected."

You have got to be kidding me?

I stared wide-eyed at the Druid. Was this some kind of joke? He wanted to deliberately put us into a state of severe hypothermia?

"That seems a bit extreme, don't you think?" Aida asked, her tone sarcastic—but her golden eyes betrayed her fear.

"Perhaps," the Druid replied. "But this water has also been infused with an herb—a highly oxidized plant that will ensure your respiratory system continues to function under the water."

"We'll be able to breathe under the water?" I asked, confused. I'd never heard of an herb that could accomplish anything *close* to that.

"Exactly."

"But that still doesn't prevent them freezing to death, does it?" Jovi questioned the Druid. I could see his body growing tense, ready to argue, and get physical if need be.

"I promise you, they will be able to withstand it," the Druid replied. "The better question is whether *you* will be able to withstand it. I need you to hold them under till they reach a state of unconsciousness, and then drag them out when I ask you to. Can you handle that?" he asked Jovi, his expression intense—I felt like it was a challenge, rather than a request, and I knew Jovi wouldn't let the Druid gain the upper hand.

"I can handle it," Jovi retorted. "I just don't know if I trust you. This method is extreme—you're basically asking me to drown my sister."

I looked down at the ice baths. I could only imagine what it was like to be submerged in them—painful beyond belief, and then later, much later, my body would heat itself as I went into hypothermic shock. I didn't relish the idea one little bit—but if this was what it was going to take to get out of here, to get back home and see our families, then it was a small price to pay.

"Jovi, it's okay," I muttered reluctantly. "We can do this."

"I hope you realize we're placing our trust in you," Aida bit out in the direction of the Druid. "Big time. And I hope for *your* sake nothing goes wrong."

Jovi shook his head, muttering expletives under his breath. Neither Field nor Phoenix looked happy with the situation, but they had obviously come to the same conclusion as I had—that it would be worth it to get home.

"And there's not another way?" Serena asked, looking pleadingly at the Druid.

"Nothing as effective," he confirmed.

"Have you done this before?" she asked.

He nodded. "Many times with my father. Please just try to trust me. We're wasting time. Believe me when I say this is the best way, and not nearly as dangerous as you think."

Serena looked skeptical but kept quiet. We all eyed the baths anxiously, until Aida, clearly tired of deliberating, took a step forward and placed her fingers in the tub closest to her. She drew them back out quickly, shaking the water off. I could tell by her expression that the water was colder than she'd initially thought it would be. From experiences of swimming in the sea in winter, I knew there was no point trying to ease ourselves in. We'd have to submerge ourselves fully in one go, or it would never happen.

"Let's get this done then," I announced, sounding way braver than I actually felt. To the sharp intakes of breath and a shocked gasp from Serena, I stepped over the side of the tub as quickly as I could and completely submerged my body into the water—with only my head above it.

Oh, my God!

My mind instantly became hysterical as my body registered the freezing temperatures. My teeth started chattering loudly in my skull. All I could do not to leap back out again was to hold onto my own body, literally freezing myself into submission. Quickly, not wanting me to be in the water any longer than I had to, Phoenix and Aida followed suit.

Phoenix gritted his teeth, exhaling his breath in a hiss as he sank into the tub. Aida wasn't so stoic—she hurled a couple of lines of abuse at the Druid, at the water, at life itself, and then sat shivering like the rest of us.

"Good. Now, the rest of you, hold them under. Their bodies will react, but you need to keep them still and completely submerged till the muscles release, and you feel them going limp."

I barely heard the instructions of the Druid, but the next moment I felt the pressure of Serena's hands on my shoulders.

"God, I'm so sorry, Vita," she whispered with a tremor in her tone as she pushed me down—my mouth, my nose, my eyes slowly sinking into the sharp freeze of the water. I struggled, my body twitching uncontrollably and fighting to get free. She held me still, and I opened my eyes, seeing her agonized expression. I couldn't hold my breath a moment longer, and my mouth yawned open in a scream, my lungs filling with water, cold cascades freezing my insides. Bubbles rose to the surface, and I thought that I was drowning.

It's gone wrong…this is all wrong!

I struggled harder in her grip, trying to tell her that she needed to let me up, or else I was going to die. More bubbles rose to the surface, but rather than passing out or my vision darkening to complete blackness, I realized I was okay. Uncomfortable certainly. The water in my lungs was the strangest sensation—like they were filled with cold air, waiting for me to exhale…except when I did, the pressure didn't release. I was breathing underwater.

Or you're dead and imagining it, I thought to myself.

That was a possibility, but my mind felt strangely alert. I looked up again, focusing on Serena. Her blue eyes rippled and distorted over the water, her mouth set in an anxious line. She kept looking forward. I guessed she was listening to the Druid's instructions. Her hands still held me firmly in their grip, but I knew she wouldn't need to keep them there for much longer. I felt like a dead weight, sinking to the bottom of the tub.

Tired, I let my eyes close, and a peaceful warmth radiated across my body.

Vita
[GRACE AND LAWRENCE'S DAUGHTER]

When I opened my eyes again, the water had gone, along with the tub and the concerned expression of my friend. I was alone, standing in the middle of a valley. The ground was dry, the earth cracked and dusty, with small islands of dried-out moss turning yellow and brown in the sunlight. The valley was about three miles wide, and went on as far as I could see in both directions. High walls stood on both sides of me. From the pattern of the rock I imagined that a river must have run here once—but a long, long time ago. The sun was at its pinnacle in the sky, large and red, burning down on the earth, with a slight breeze that knocked dust up in my face, irritating my eyes with grit particles.

Am I having a vision?

It didn't feel like the last one, where the images had felt like they were appearing in my mind and I could watch them like I would a TV. This was completely different. I was part of this, feeling the sunshine and everything else as if it was real. I stepped forward, knocking a small rock with my foot. It moved, and I could feel the crumbling earth beneath the soles of my feet.

I looked around. What was it that I was meant to be seeing? The place was completely silent, to the extent that I felt like I was the only person on the planet. Not knowing what else to do, I kept walking. The ground hurt my feet, while the sun burnt my bare arms and the top of my head. I idly wondered if I could actually get sunburned, whether I'd come out of the semi-conscious state in the basement with a peeling nose and a killer headache.

"Hello?" I called out. The sound of my own voice was strange, and it echoed across the valley, a lone, weak voice that went unanswered. I was starting to become afraid, wary of my own lengthening shadow on the ground, and the oppressive silence that blanketed everything. It reminded me of the journey from the portal to Sherus's fire star in the In-Between, those moments of deafening silence that made you think you were going half-mad, that you would lose your mind completely if it didn't come to an end soon.

Shielding my eyes from the sun's glare, I took another look around. It was difficult to see—the heat created a hazy fuzz that rippled in the distance, but there did seem to be a figure up ahead. Whatever it was, it wasn't moving, which suggested it was more likely a tree or rock, but I called out anyway.

"Hello? Can you hear me? Anyone?"

The figure might have moved—I couldn't really tell—but no one returned my call. I started to pick up my pace, stumbling over the rocks and gritting my teeth as stones bit into my feet.

I could feel perspiration running down my back, my hair sticking to my temples and neck. It was almost enough to make me long for the ice-cold bath that was waiting for me back in the basement. Ahead of me, the figure was starting to become clearer, and I decided that it was definitely human, or human-shaped, at least.

Please be someone I know.

"Jovi?" I called out hopefully, knowing the moment that his name left my lips it was a dumb conclusion. Jovi would have answered back, and come toward me. Still, maybe in a vision that stuff was different. The figure was about the right height for Jovi, and had the same dark hair, though as I got closer, I realized that there was a lot *less* hair than Jovi had. He stood with his back facing me, not moving.

I reached about a yard away before I realized who it was, and I came to a standstill.

Bijarki?

He was the last person I expected to see. What was he doing in my vision? He was wearing different clothes to the ones I had previously seen him in, a loose white shirt that fluttered in the breeze and khaki-colored cotton trousers. They must have come from the plantation house, as they were certainly of that period, and I couldn't imagine that he would have gotten clothes like that anywhere else.

"Bijarki?" I called out his name. This time he turned and faced me, his face splitting into a smile.

"Are you ready?" he asked.

"For what?"

I took a step backward, unnerved by his gaze. It looked so intimate, like he *knew* me somehow, not just as one of the Oracles that the Druid was looking after, but as a friend or a…*Don't go there.*

"Vita, we need to hurry," he admonished. "We don't have time to mess around."

He held out his hand toward me, palm open, waiting for me to take it. I stared at the taut muscle of his forearm, how his skin had a slight silver sheen to it, like his bones were made of metal. For some unaccountable reason, I felt a strong urge to take his hand, to discover what it would feel like to have my palm against his. I looked up, into his eyes, seeing an urgency reflected there, an impatience because I wouldn't do as he asked.

"Vita, please," he begged.

I placed my hand in his, and the vision vanished.

Without time enough to blink, I was somewhere else— this time standing in the corner of a large room. At one end, there was a large door, guarded by two vile Destroyers. They sat atop their winged horses, their tails wrapped tightly around the middle of their horses' bellies, holding them upright. Each of them held a pointed spear, the tips of the wood seeping with a bright purple liquid I recognized from the jungle. Their black eyes stared unseeingly ahead, and the only movement they made was the occasional flare of their nostrils, as if they were constantly sniffing out scents in the room. I didn't know if I was visible to them or not, but I tried to remain perfectly still, not wanting to take any chances.

At the other end of the room, there was a giant rock. It was black, like volcanic stone, and sprawled out, filling the entire width of the room on either side. In the center of the rock sat another Destroyer. He was no larger than the other two who stood guard, but his presence seemed to fill the room entirely. He had long, dark hair, spilling down to his waist, and a thick beard that was braided at the end, ending in a perfect point between the well-defined pectorals on his chest.

He was such an all-consuming sight that I'd almost failed to notice the small figure standing in front of him, looking slight and waif-like in comparison. I blinked a few times, opening my mouth in a gasp of surprise as I recognized the figure as myself.

When neither of the guards so much as turned their heads at my sharp intake of breath, I started to move forward, testing my theory that they couldn't see me. Relieved when they still didn't notice me, and neither did the Destroyer on the throne, I got closer, wanting to hear the exchange between my 'other' self and the creature on the throne.

"You are mine now," he hissed. "And you will be mine for an eternity. It will be up to you how it is spent—in my good graces, receiving all the gifts you could possibly imagine, or in disfavor, a lonely life floating in a bowl, seeing a world that you will never be part of again."

"Then I choose disfavor," the 'other' me spat back. My hands were held in fists at my sides, with two bright spots on either cheek. "I would rather die of loneliness than spend a second in your company!"

The Destroyer, who I was now convinced was Azazel himself, leaned back on his throne and laughed.

"Does he mean that little to you?" he asked, languorously stroking his beard. I watched as my face blanched and my entire body started to tremble. Who was he referring to? It had obviously caused me to have a visceral reaction, so the person he was threatening—besides me—was obviously important—it could have been any one of my friends, but the mention of a 'he' automatically made me think of some romantic attachment…but perhaps that was a misleading assumption.

Before any more of the vision could unfold, the scene vanished again—this time, very much against my will.

The next vision was upon me before I could recover from the last. I felt like I was still trying to hold on to the throne room, desperately wanting to know what had happened, what my decision had been, but I was already somewhere else, standing beneath a star-studded sky, the lights so bright that they felt like they were near enough to reach out and touch.

My heart felt like it had stopped beating in my chest as I greedily tried to take in my surroundings. Without a shadow of a doubt, it was the most beautiful, awe-inspiring sight I had ever witnessed.

I was standing on a mountain, and must have been so high up I was practically touching the heavens. I could see galaxies unfurling in the distance—pink, purple and blue hues glowing in the night's sky, as if the entire cosmos was laid out in front of me. Its beauty made my throat tighten, keeping down a well of emotion that was building up inside of me.

My vision started to blur, and I hastily wiped at my eyes. Refocusing on where I was standing, I realized I was on the edge of a cliff, perilously close to the edge. Crouching down, ignoring the biting cold of the wind that whipped around me, I crawled forward, trying to see what lay over the side.

Directly beneath me was another cliff edge, and beyond that, nothing but darkness. I turned my attention back to the second ledge, where there was a bright light coming from beneath a large slab of stone. From my vantage point, I couldn't understand what the construction was, but the light was enough that I could see a small path leading down to the second level. Shuffling backward from the edge, I turned toward the left, where I could see the start of the path. As I moved off the rock, I felt soft grass beneath my feet, wet with dew. I moved slowly along the path, suddenly in no hurry to get where I was going, still entranced by the sky and its glinting stars, enjoying the cool of the night.

As I approached the light, I realized that the slab of stone I'd seen from above was supported by columns, and in the middle of the structure was a large glass sphere where the light was emanating from. The grass of the pathway ended, and I was back walking on rock, making my way toward the sphere. I started to hurry as I saw a figure floating inside it.

The Oracle.

Her white hair streamed out behind her while her frail

body appeared to float about in mid-air, until I realized that the sphere was full of water. She turned to face me, those impossibly pale blue eyes meeting mine.

"Vita." She whispered my name, and like the time she'd reached out to me in the bathroom mirror, I heard her voice inside my head, disorientating me completely so I almost stumbled and fell flat across the ground. Regaining my balance, I rushed forward, reaching out to touch the glass of her prison.

"Can you hear me?" I asked urgently, looking around to see if I could use something to break the glass. Before she could reply, footsteps came from behind me. Both the Oracle and I turned in the direction of the sound, and my friends, led by the Druid, rushed down the footpath that I'd used only seconds earlier.

Before they could reach us, a horrifying scream split through the air. I yelled out, putting my arms up to stop the Druid and everyone else approaching, but they couldn't see me. Out of the darkness, the Destroyers rose up from the abyss over the side of the cliff, their horses screeching and snorting as the Destroyers raised their spears.

"Stop!" I cried out, running toward the others.

The Druid turned to face the creatures, shoving Serena

behind him as he did so. Field flew up into the air, wielding two swords, their blades aimed directly at the Destroyers. One of them threw his spear. It missed the Druid by inches, but then Serena screamed. I turned to her, running as quickly as I could to reach her. The Druid moved forward to attack, and I saw Jovi, held up by Serena, a spear protruding from his chest.

I woke up in the ice-cold tub, screaming.

Aida
[Victoria and Bastien's daughter]

I clamped my eyes shut, hoping for oblivion to come as quickly as possible. I couldn't stand the cold of the water a second longer; it felt like my whole body had been frozen rigid, while my blood boiled in fury and frustration, wanting out. Wanting never to have agreed to this dumb, dangerous idea.

Please…please, make it stop!

It felt like an eternity until my prayers were answered, though in reality it had probably only been a couple of seconds before a slow heat burned its way through me, my body's tremors and shakes subsiding.

I opened my eyes, discovering that the basement had been replaced by dense and colorful jungle. I inhaled deeply—the humid, hot air was better than the musty staleness of the house—and looked around me.

I wasn't alone.

The vision had placed me in the center of a clearing, and everywhere I looked I could see men, standing around in small groups, all with the silvery skin of the incubus. In all honesty, it was a bit like wandering backstage at a catwalk show at a men's fashion week. There were men who must have been older than seventy (by human standards) present, but they were so inhumanly beautiful, their age appeared to add to their beauty, not detract from it. I started to move around, quickly realizing that I was invisible to them, and tried to listen in to some of their conversations. I was also curious as to why there weren't any women around…was this some kind of army regiment? They were all wearing the same military-style clothing that Bijarki wore, so perhaps my guess was correct.

I sidled up to the nearest group, daring to take a seat by one of the oldest-looking incubi there. His hair was wild and unkempt, with ropes of different colored beads hanging from his neck. The top he wore was stained with mud and sweat, his boots so worn the soles looked like they would fall to pieces with the next step he took.

"It is insanity, and worse, a death wish!" the older man barked at a younger one, spitting seed cases from his lips. "How can you think of betraying us that way? Oh, yes, it's an 'us'—your sons and daughters, and their sons and daughters!"

The younger man shook his head, his lips curled in disdain. "What else do you think we can do? The Druids have all surrendered. There is no one left. We are incapable of standing against Azazel. What would your plan be? Do we make ourselves extinct, Father?"

"Better to die in honor than to live in shame," the older man retorted, his fist clenching as if he wanted to smash sense into his son.

"There's no honor in death!" cried the son. "I'm talking about buying us time. We can't stand against the Destroyers now, but we can stand another day, when the time is right. When we have a chance."

"And when will that be?" the father retorted, scooping more seeds out from a woven hemp bag at his feet and knocking them back into his mouth.

"One Druid still lives," the incubus replied softly, looking intently at his father and then glancing around the clearing to see if anyone else had overheard him. Most of the groups were intent on their own conversations, and few seemed to be taking interest in the heated exchange.

"In his bubble of safety!" the man roared. "He's no good to any of us, and neither is your brother. Better that we forget them, better that we forge our own futures than rely on a single Druid to save us!"

The younger incubus shook his head. "Your way leaves us with no future. We will just be dead men."

He turned his back on his father, his head bent in sorrow, all the anger and disdain wiped from him. I started to follow him, wishing I could say something that might help, or to comfort him at least, but as soon as I had taken the first step, the vision started to fade.

I was transported to the next vision. My stomach gave a sickening lurch, a bit like I was plummeting in an elevator, and then settled again, leaving me feeling slightly nauseous as I tried to get my bearings. This time, the vivid light of the jungle had gone, and I was standing in gloom at one end of a long, low-ceilinged tunnel. Behind me there was a dead end, but cut into the stone was a barred window—a small semi-circle that let in light. I peered outside, seeing nothing other than a huge stone wall a few yards away, and above that, only empty sky.

I turned back around, looking toward the far end of the gloomy tunnel. Arched entrances led off this one, but in the distance, I could see nothing more than darkness. The tunnel must go on for miles.

I brushed my fingers along the wall, my skin crawling at the cold dampness. I hoped this vision would end soon—the previous one was far preferable to this. I felt like I was in a prison of some sort, because I couldn't understand why else anyone would build a place like this. I couldn't imagine anybody, supernatural or otherwise, thinking that this place was habitable.

Walking forward, I instinctively tried to make as little noise as possible despite knowing that it made little difference, no one would be able to hear or see me anyway. I came to the first tunnel that led off the one I was on, but nothing but more darkness lay ahead. I kept going, coming to the second archway. This one looked more promising. It led downward, rather than straight along, and I thought I could detect faint glows of light coming from its depths.

There were no stairs to navigate, only a consistent slope of the ground which I discovered in places was almost impossibly steep. I kept going, determined to find something of use before the vision faded.

Soon I could hear voices, and the ground started to level out beneath me. I had slowed down, more cautious now that I knew I wasn't alone, but in the next moment, a howl of pain ricocheted along the tunnel. I stopped dead in my tracks. The cry was so pain-filled and anguished that I could swear I felt it in my bones. I bent double, catching my breath as the cry went on and on.

"Answer us!" a voice hissed, halting the last notes of the cry.

"I can't! I promise you—I *can't!*" The reply was choked, torn from the speaker's throat with as much pain as their howls had been.

Desperate to know what was going on, I continued to creep along the tunnel, heading for the light at the far end. When I reached the archway, I backed into the wall to peer around the stone.

The archway led into a small, circular room, the ceiling domed and just as low as the tunnel walls. The light was coming from a small fire in the middle of the room, and behind its red and yellow flames I could make out the figure of a man, stretched out on a stone table, his arms tied to one end, his legs tied to another. Leering over his exposed torso was another man—his chest broad, his arms muscular, one of which was covered in black tattooed lines ringed around his bicep. His eyes were black, completely black, with no irises or pupils. The man moved suddenly, shifting his position till he was at the top of the table, leaning over the prisoner's head. As he moved, I noticed that he had no legs—instead, a thick, scaly tail wormed around the circumference of the room.

A Destroyer!

I recognized his species from the painting that Serena had shown us in the Druid's house. In the artist's depiction, the creature had looked monstrous—in real life, up close, it was much worse. I could practically feel the evil radiating off his skin. The room smelt like death, pungent and foul, as if the blood of a million different victims had already been soaked into the floor.

"We know they're here," the Destroyer whispered. "*He* knows they crossed. It will only be a matter of time… surely your life is worth more than this?"

The Destroyer lifted his own finger to his mouth. He

bared his teeth, and I watched as two of them elongated and became fangs. He pierced the skin of his own finger, blood running down his hand. Next, he placed the finger on the exposed flesh of the man tied to the table, running it along his chest.

The man screamed again, rising off the table as his spine twisted and arched, desperate to escape. I smelled burning flesh. I turned away, unable to watch someone endure so much. I didn't know what exactly was causing the pain, but I suspected it was a venom of some kind that had been produced by the Destroyer's fangs.

I shuddered.

"I don't *know*," the prisoner replied helplessly when his cries had subsided once more. "If I knew anything I would tell you, but I know nothing of a new Oracle."

"Oracl*es*," the Destroyer corrected him with a furious hiss. He turned away from the prisoner in disgust, slamming his fist into the stone wall. It shook from the force of the impact, sending dust scattering from the ceiling.

"This is inconvenient," the Destroyer snarled to himself.

"Let me go." The prisoner trembled. "I can find out more. I-I can hunt them, find out where they are…"

The Destroyer looked disdainfully down at his prisoner.

I tried to get a good look at him too. If the Destroyer agreed to his bargain, then this man would soon come searching for us. I started to move closer, holding my breath, terrified that the Destroyer might be able to sense my presence, even if he couldn't see me.

The fire produced a lot of smoke, which made it difficult to make out the person on the table behind its flames, but I could see a fan of dark hair and a distinguished-looking profile, with a Roman nose and square jaw. His face was covered in dirt, soot and perspiration, hair matted to his forehead.

"And we would trust you to do such a thing?" the Destroyer questioned him, his tone sneering.

"Yes! I know what he is capable of!" the man cried, moving his head about wildly in order to catch the Destroyer's eye. "Let me serve you!"

I felt a wave of nausea swimming in my gut, and I knew the vision was about to vanish. I took one last look at the prisoner on the table as the scene before me vanished.

Gasping, I stumbled into the next vision, glad to be moving away from that place. I sighed in relief as I saw the familiar figures of my friends standing in the basement.

"Thank God," I groaned, walking up to Serena. "That was *horrific.*"

I frowned, reaching out to hold her arm, but she paid absolutely no attention to me whatsoever. When my fingertips reached her bare arm, I felt her skin, warm and solid, but she still paid no attention to me.

What is happening?

I followed her gaze, and then jumped back in horror. Her eyes were fixed on the metal bathtub. Lying still, and completely submerged under the water, was *me.*

"When do we pull them out?" Serena asked the Druid, her voice desperate. Her hands clutched the sides of the tub, her knuckles white.

"When they're ready," he replied, peering over another of the tubs, staring down at Phoenix, who lay still like I did.

Wake me up now!

I wanted out of this. I felt like the vision was more like a nightmare than anything else—like experiencing sleep paralysis, when all I wanted to do was wake up. Beneath the water my body looked like a dead, drowned thing. My eyes were closed, my hair wafting in the water like seaweed.

I moved past Serena, wondering if I could somehow climb back into my body…I had seen that in a movie once, with ghosts re-inhabiting their bodies to animate themselves. Would that work? I stood bent over the tub, ready to step into it, when Vita suddenly sat bolt upright in the water. Her eyes were wide open, and she started to scream.

PHOENIX
[HAZEL AND TEJUS'S SON]

My head was pounding, my vision blurring gray at the edges, as if I'd been heavily syphoned from. I kept my eyes closed, waiting for the feeling to subside. When the ache left my temples, I opened my eyes and looked around.

I was standing in a room of the house—the room that the Druid habitually sat in, with the door that led down to the basement. I recognized the windows, and the view out onto the gardens, but everything else was very different. The fire wasn't lit, for one, and all signs of shabby decay had long gone. The wallpaper was a dusty pale pink. Heavy velvet curtains were drawn aside, letting the sunlight stream in from outside. On either side of the fireplace were bookcases, containing neatly bound leather books, the kind kept more for show than actual reading. The room was also full of furniture—small tables covered in decorative porcelain figurines and lace table mats. The room smelled of polish and freshly varnished wood.

As I stood in the sunlight, trying to understand how this could possibly be a vision—it felt more like I was looking backward, not forward into the future—a woman strode purposefully into the room.

Her hair was tightly drawn back into a bun, and her clothes were old-fashioned—a simple dress with a small bustle at the waist, and a white pinafore covering it. Ignoring me completely, she walked over to the fireplace, and, kneeling down, proceeded to sweep up the ashes fallen from the grate.

"Hello?" I called, wondering if she'd seen me.

I was ignored, and, approaching the fireplace, I realized she had no idea I was there. Clearly, this was a benefit of the visions—never having to explain how I'd just miraculously appeared in a place, or what I was doing there.

I kept watching the woman as she cleared the ash,

noticing the perspiration building on her forehead and the attractive silhouette of her face, before I eventually realized she was blind. It hadn't been immediately noticeable because of the effectiveness of her work and the sure way in which she'd crossed the room—it was only after some time that I realized her sight was fixed at a point ahead of her, not on the task she was performing.

"Are you going to be down there all day?" A sharp voice pierced through the room. I turned to see another woman at the door, much older than the blind woman, grossly overweight, with a rolling pin clutched in her chubby hand.

"I'm sorry," the blind woman replied meekly, brushing faster.

I frowned at the woman in the doorway, wishing I could say something. The fact that she could sweep a fireplace at all was a feat in itself.

"Lord above," the large woman cried, "what she and the master were thinking when they hired a blind scrap like you, I'll never know!" She waved the rolling pin in the air, tutting dismissively at the woman before storming off—no doubt to berate someone else. I strode swiftly to the doorway, noticing the frantic action that lay outside the room. There were servants everywhere, dressed in a finer manner than the blind woman, but just as preoccupied in their work, carrying tables and chairs along the hallway, and sweeping and dusting the main entrance.

I was about to leave the blind woman and investigate when she cried out. Turning, I saw her bent double in pain. The dustpan brush tumbled to the floor, sending soot flying everywhere. I hurried over to her, forgetting I couldn't help, but froze on the spot as she arched her back in pain. Shadows started to appear on her skin, taking the form of strange runes flittering across her face and arms. Her eyes rolled back in her head, her mouth open and gasping for breath.

She was an Oracle! The realization surprised me and I took a closer look at her figure, noting she had no breasts— suggesting an absence of reproductive organs that I knew the Oracle twins also lacked. But what was the daughter of a jinni and a witch doing here? Living as a lowly servant?

Before I could discover more about what was going on here, I felt the headache return, my vision blurring, and the room starting to spin.

When I opened my eyes, and the headache receded once more, I found myself back in the same house. This time, it looked more familiar—the wallpaper was starting to age, and I was on the second floor where our bedrooms were, surrounded by the same oddities that existed there now— the stuffed animals, the piles of books and worn-out carpet. As I was looking around, noting the still silence of the house, a young boy ran out from one of the rooms, clutching a leather-bound notebook, the same book Serena had found. It was the diary of the Oracle "Elissa", and he waved it about in the air, laughing as he tore past me.

"You little monster!" A laughing voice echoed down the hallway, and the same woman I'd seen in the last vision— the Oracle—stepped out from the same room the kid had just exited. Her face was lit up in a smile, the stern hairstyle gone, leaving tumbling auburn locks flowing across her shoulders. She started to chase the boy, running past me. I wanted to reach out and stop her, suddenly realizing she was no longer blind. Her eyes were fixed on the corridor, but I was absolutely sure she was taking it all in. I followed the pair of them into another room—the last in the hallway, where the girls were currently sleeping.

"Give it back!" the Oracle exclaimed.

The boy dove under the sheets of the bed, hiding beneath them as he giggled. The Oracle leapt on the bed, throwing back the sheets. She grabbed the boy, tickling his stomach and making mock-growling noises as he laughed helplessly and called out for someone to save him.

"Elissa's a monster!" he crowed. "Help me!"

"Better a monster than a thief, little man!" She laughed, blowing raspberries into the back of his neck. I smiled despite myself, glad that the Oracle was laughing, and clearly very much in love with the little boy. Somehow her circumstances must have changed—whether it was because she'd regained her sight, or something else, I couldn't tell.

"A thief?" A man's voice sounded from the doorway. I spun around to see a figure who looked remarkably like the Druid, leaning against the doorframe, his expression amused as he watched the play-fighting continue. "Say it isn't true, Draven—have you been taking things from Elissa again?"

The boy looked up, smiling broadly at the man. "Only because she wouldn't play with me!" the young boy retorted, as if his argument was perfectly fair.

The Oracle and the man looked at one another knowingly.

"I think you should apologize, and return what you've taken," the man replied, coming over to sit on the bed. The boy heaved himself against the man's back, still clutching the notebook.

"But Father, then she'll keep writing, and she won't come outside!" he complained dramatically.

"Have you even asked me yet?" teased the Oracle.

The boy stopped his theatrics and turned to the Oracle, as if the thought hadn't even occurred to him.

"Will you come outside?" he asked.

"If you give me back my diary, yes." She smiled.

The boy hastily shoved the book back into her waiting hands, and jumped down from the bed.

"The apology?" his father prompted, holding him back from running out of the room.

"Sorry, Elissa," the boy called out, already halfway through the door. The Oracle got up to follow him, doing her best to neaten the rumpled sheets. The man clasped her hand as she went to follow the boy.

"Are you happy here, Elissa?" the man asked, the amusement gone from his face as he looked up at her from the bed with a searching gaze.

"You know I am," the Oracle replied softly. "Happier than I can ever remember being."

The man nodded, satisfied.

"Good. Let me know if there's anything you need," he replied.

The Oracle shook her head.

"There's nothing that I want for, Almus."

Almus. The Druid's father. I recalled the name from the diary Serena was reading. I stared at the now empty doorway in astonishment. Was that small boy really the Druid—and his name was Draven? I looked around, and at the dress of the Oracle and Almus, both looking like they were in an eighteenth-century costume drama.... the Druid must be centuries old. What had happened to the Oracle, Elissa? Why was she no longer in the house? Had she met the same fate as the Druid's father, or perhaps worse, been captured by Azazel?

The Oracle left the room, blushing slightly as she left. I could tell there was something between the two of them— not a fully developed romantic relationship, not yet, but there was certainly one developing.

Before I could give it more thought, my headache returned, and I knew it was time for me to move on.

The next vision took me outdoors, standing alone in the middle of a large garden. I turned around to see the façade of the plantation house. I must have been at the front entrance, where none of us had explored yet. I could see the grandeur of the building in its fullness here—the classic columns that ran the height of the building, and the porch that ran its length, shaded by large magnolia trees. There was also a second-floor balcony I hadn't realized existed, backing onto the front rooms of the house. Once again, due to the pristine condition of the plaster and stone, I figured I must be in the past—no doubt most of the porch would be rotten and crumbling now like the rest of the interior.

I looked around, trying to work out what I was supposed to be seeing. I was starting to understand that each vision held a clue of some kind—leading to what, I wasn't quite sure, but there was a definite message and order to the visions I'd been receiving.

No one was around, and I started to walk up to the porch, wondering if I was meant to go inside the house. As soon as my foot touched the first step up to the main door, I turned back around. There was still nothing to see, but my eyes were drawn back to the tree I'd first been standing by.

There wasn't anything to distinguish it from the others that surrounded the house, except that its boughs seemed to reach a little wider than most. It was in full bloom, its pale pink flower petals covering the grass where it grew as well as its branches. I started to make my way back, noticing for the first time there was a faint breeze in the air, sending some of the petals scattering and dancing toward me.

When I reached its trunk, I placed my hand on the bark of one of the branches. The tree was warm, probably from the sun. I removed my hand, picking up one of the petals that had flown onto my chest. I studied it, but it seemed ordinary. I dropped the petal, wondering why on earth I was being shown a tree. I was absolutely certain this was what I was meant to be seeing…but I just didn't understand *why*.

"Give me a break," I mumbled to the sky. "What am I supposed to be doing?"

Only the breeze answered, sending another scatter of petals my way. My headache returned, and I sighed—partly in frustration, partly in relief. The boringness of the vision, and the absolute silence from the house, had started to unnerve me.

SERENA
[HAZEL AND TEJUS'S DAUGHTER]

Vita sat up in the tub and screamed. Her eyes were wide with fear, her entire body shaking, whether from the freezing-cold temperatures of the tub or from what she'd seen in her vision, I didn't know.

"Vita!" I cried, hauling her up and out of the ice water. Jovi, Field and Bijarki were by my side in a second—Bijarki with a towel that he instantly wrapped around her shaking body, moving us aside. She leaned on him, but her stare was fixed on Jovi, darting over his body until she started to calm down. Her breathing was labored, and Bijarki held her more tightly. I would have objected to him touching her that way had I not been absolutely sure that she needed body heat. Still, I would have preferred it to have been Jovi or Field.

"Vita, what happened?" I asked, cupping her face in my hands as I forced her to focus on me.

"The vision," she replied, trembling. "It was horrible…I'm still, eugh—It was just…*bad*." She started to realize who was holding her so intimately, and extracted herself from Bijarki's grip. The incubus watched her with a frown, but let her move away from him and took a step back.

"She needs a hot shower," Jovi announced, looking around for some more towels.

"No," the Druid replied. "It will cause chilblains, she needs to warm up slowly. We'll go upstairs when the others wake up, it shouldn't be long now."

Jovi looked like he wanted to object, but stayed silent—I agreed with the Druid, a sudden blast of heat would be painful for her. I stepped in, warning the others to give her some space, and held her tightly in the towel. It was the best we could do for now.

I anxiously waited for the others to wake up. Would they

be as traumatized as Vita when they did? I watched their unnaturally still bodies, silently praying that they would open their eyes.

Aida was next.

She burst up and out of the water so suddenly, I almost jumped out of my skin.

"What the hell!" she cried out, looking wildly around her as Vita had, but her features were set in fury, not fear. Her muscles were taut, her body crouched into a predatory pose.

"Aida, it's just us." Jovi held out his hand to help her out of the tub. Her golden eyes widened, and after a few seconds she clutched on to him, allowing her brother to maneuver her onto the ground. He silently handed her a towel, and she took it gratefully.

My eyes met Jovi's. I hadn't expected this—the visions had affected our friends far more than either of us had anticipated. He held his sister tightly to him, and muttered something under his breath.

Field remained looking over Phoenix's tub, but repeatedly glanced at Aida and Vita, clearly eager for my brother to wake up so we could all get out of here. Vita's shakes seemed to be intensifying, and now I was sure it was down to a dangerously low body temperature.

"I need to get out of here," Aida pleaded. "Please, Jovi."

"Wait," the Druid replied, moving over to Phoenix's tub. "Field, help me drag him up. He's stayed under too long."

Field instantly yanked Phoenix up, lifting him clear of the tub. My brother coughed a few times, his body spasming as he tried to fight off Field. The Hawk wouldn't let him, holding on tightly as my brother twisted in his grip.

"Wake up!" Field yelled at him, shaking him by the shoulders. Phoenix took a large, shuddering breath and stopped struggling. He looked around at us all, and I could see his muscles start to relax as he recognized where he was.

"Sorry." He turned to Field, who handed him a towel and shook his head.

"Don't be. Are you all right?"

"Been better," my brother replied, looking back at the tub in confusion. He then turned to Vita and Aida, his eyes widening as he took in their shaking bodies and their still-wild eyes.

"Upstairs," the Druid commanded. I didn't hesitate to follow him out of the room, still clutching Vita to me as we ascended the staircase. The Druid came to a stop in the living room, where the fire was blazing. I walked Vita over to the chair in front of the fire—there was easily enough space for both her and Aida. Jovi joined me, helping his sister sit down.

"Phoenix, stand by the fire," I urged my brother. He was standing in the doorway from the basement, looking around the living room in a gaze close to fascination.

"Phoenix?" I prompted him.

"Yeah, sorry," he replied, moving to the fireplace and standing by the chair. I looked at the Druid. I was desperate to know what they'd seen—but I didn't want to pressure them either, it had obviously been an ordeal. Bijarki stood in the corner of the room, looking over at the two girls on the armchair. He looked pale and worried. I wasn't sure how I felt about his concern—was it directed at Vita? Or all three of them? If the latter, I would consider his concern more genuine…I caught the incubus's eye, and he frowned, irritation flickering across his expression, and then moved across the room to stand by the Druid.

"Can you tell us about the visions?" the Druid asked. "It's important we know what you saw."

Vita nodded, standing up from the chair and moving closer to the fire.

"There's a lot I don't understand," she whispered.

"I know," the Druid replied. "That's fine. Hopefully, we

can piece together anything you don't understand."

"Okay," Vita replied, taking a deep breath. "I had three visions—one was in an empty valley, it was huge and I was walking through it…" She paused, looking down at the floor. "And then I saw a figure up ahead, but I didn't recognize who it was."

Her glance swept the room, and then returned to the floor. I had known Vita since I was little, and I knew something wasn't quite right…she was leaving something out, but I didn't know why. I swiftly looked over at the Druid, to see if he'd noticed anything was amiss, but he was just looking at Vita with an inquisitive expression.

"Then the vision changed, and I was in a room with three Destroyers—one of them Azazel."

I gasped at this—no wonder she'd woken up screaming.

"He was threatening me—with the life of someone else, but I didn't know who. Then the vision changed again, and I saw the Nevertide Oracle. We were all trying to save her…but then the Destroyers came." She shook her head, as if trying to shake away the vision. All of us fell silent, except the Druid, who continued to question her on the specifics. The conversation didn't return to the valley though, and the figure she'd seen. When Vita had finished being interrogated, it was Aida's turn. She told us, in a quavering voice I hardly recognized as belonging to my friend, what she'd seen.

"So there might be someone hunting us down, along with the Destroyers?" I asked when she'd finished.

Aida nodded. "I didn't hear what the Destroyer's decision was—the man he was torturing might be dead," she replied.

"Can you describe the man?" the Druid asked.

Aida nodded, recalling the vision as best she could. When she had finished, the Druid ran a hand through his hair, his face twisted in an expression of disgust.

"Do you know who it might be?" I asked.

"Another Druid, who must have survived," he replied shortly. "But I'm not entirely sure who. There are a few families…a few Druid families, that managed to escape the first sweep of Azazel's annihilation of our kind, but that was a long time ago now. I'm not sure who's left."

"And the incubi?" I asked Bijarki. "Who are they?"

"An army. The last that we have. And by the sounds of it, they are not going to be around for much longer." The incubus turned his attention to the Druid. "It sounds like Kristos's father and brother. Without Kristos's support, they won't wait for us—they will attack Azazel's Destroyers and be wiped out like all before them."

I recalled that Kristos had been the incubus who had died in the jungle the day we came across Bijarki while attempting to flee the house. Bijarki had also mentioned that his own father had betrayed the incubi, siding with the Destroyers. If that was the case, then I doubted Bijarki could do much to persuade them not to fight. I suddenly felt a wave of pity for the incubi. It sounded like things were desperate for all the species of Eritopia.

"But these things are happening in the future, right?" I clarified. Maybe there was time to stop the incubus armies.

The Druid shook his head. "I'm not entirely sure of that. Phoenix, can you tell us what you saw?"

"This house," my brother replied evenly. "I had three visions as well, but they were all here. I saw an Oracle named Elissa, first as a servant girl, surrounded by other servants, and then later, when she was sharing this house with someone called Almus and a young boy."

I glanced quickly at my brother. He gave me a small, barely perceptible nod. He wouldn't tell the Druid about the diary. I turned my attention back to the Druid, interested to see how he would react to this vision—I was convinced that Almus was his father.

"Elissa," he replied softly, his gaze miles away. His features softened for a moment, and then he cleared his throat. "Yes. She was the Oracle who lived here with my father and me, long before the Nevertide Oracle ventured into the In-Between. Interesting that you should see her…"

"Your name is Draven, isn't it?" Phoenix prompted.

The Druid's face went still, holding Phoenix's gaze, then he nodded. "That is my name, but that's beside the point… Did you see anything else?"

"A tree," Phoenix replied, frowning. "But nothing happened—it was just a magnolia tree, outside the house."

Draven – thank God we finally had a name for him—nodded slowly.

"I think what's happening here is that your visions have somehow divided," Draven replied, completely ignoring the matter of the tree. "Vita's visions took place in the future, Phoenix's in the past—which makes me assume that Aida's visions, especially as she saw Vita emerging from the bath, are of the present."

"Has that ever happened before?" I asked, stunned.

"Not that I know of," Draven replied. "But then no other Oracle has passed her gift on to another—nor has there ever been an Oracle who was descended from an Ancient."

"But the future can change, can't it?" Vita burst out, pallor returning to her features.

"Yes, it can change," Draven reassured her. "Depending on decisions and actions changing in the present. It is perhaps fortunate that the visions have been divided between you this way—it means we will be better able to isolate what is happening now, what happened in the past, and what may be to come. In most Oracles, it is very difficult to separate the three."

Vita sank back down into the armchair, gathering up her knees and clutching them to her chest. She had definitely omitted something from her visions—her panic was obvious, and I wondered if she had also left out details of the Destroyer attack she saw. She had claimed she only saw them appear, but now I wasn't so sure.

"I think that's enough for today." I turned to Draven, who looked like he was about to disagree with me, until he saw the warning flash in my eyes. My friends had been through enough. Anything else could wait until tonight or tomorrow. All three of them looked completely exhausted.

"Fine," Draven replied. "Get some rest. We will resume

training tomorrow." He walked toward the door and then waited, turning to Bijarki with an arched brow when the incubus failed to follow him.

"Right," Bijarki muttered, taking one last look in Vita's direction before following Draven from the room.

Vita

[Grace and Lawrence's daughter]

I should have said something.

Should I?

I just didn't know. I hoped I'd given the Druid enough information to know what lay ahead, without having to go into the specifics. And if my visions were open to change, then wouldn't telling everyone about Jovi just worry them needlessly? On the other hand, maybe it was important to be fully aware of the dangers…what might potentially lie ahead. But perhaps now wasn't the right time—maybe I could tell them later. The visions didn't take place here, so there was no need to say anything until we left the house…maybe that was the best solution.

Keeping quiet about Bijarki had been more of a self-preservation tactic. I was so embarrassed to have had a vision about him—how would I explain what he was doing there? Why it had felt so intimate, as if we were far closer than I ever wanted to be to the incubus?

Serena was the only one who had noticed something was wrong. I'd seen the way that she looked at me—she'd known I was leaving something out.

"Do you want to get some air?" I asked Aida after Draven left the room.

"Yeah, good idea." Aida got up off the chair. Serena looked like she wanted to follow us, but Phoenix took her aside instead. We were followed out of the room by Jovi and Field. Together we all made our way to the greenhouse, and then out into the garden.

It felt good to be outside—the living room had started to grow stuffy, but at least my body temperature had returned to normal. I sat down on the grass, and Aida followed me. My pajamas were still damp, but the sunshine would dry them out in a matter of moments. I lay back on the grass, suddenly overwhelmed by exhaustion.

"I guess we can't argue anymore about whether or not we're Oracles." Aida sighed. "But what's that going to mean? Are we going to go blind? Have shadows running across our skin?" She hesitated, thinking of something else.

"Reproductive organs?" I asked, guessing where her mind had gone.

"Yeah. That won't happen though, right?" she replied softly.

"Don't worry about that," Jovi interrupted, collapsing on the ground next to us. "I don't think anything about you three is normal in Oracle terms. And remember what Phoenix said about Elissa—she obviously found a way to regain her sight."

I nodded, only partly reassured.

"She's the Oracle who wrote the diary, isn't she?" I asked.

"I think so," Field replied. "It's probably what Phoenix and Serena are talking about now. Hopefully the diary will have answers about how she overcame some of the side-effects."

"I'm starting to think this gift is more of a curse," Aida grumbled.

"*Starting* to think?" I replied in astonishment. "I've been thinking that ever since we arrived."

"Well, I thought it might be quite cool...who doesn't want to see the future? But I have definitely got the dud gift. Who wants to see the *present*? It's totally useless."

I'd be happy not to see the future, I thought.

"It's not useless," I replied instead. "It's helpful. Especially when we can't leave the house. And just think how good it will be to GASP when we get home—you can see an attack, and then it will take seconds for the witches to travel somewhere. You might end up saving a lot of lives, Aida."

The girl smiled reluctantly. "I guess I didn't really think about it that way."

"Because you're never happy with what you have," Jovi replied dryly. I laughed, recognizing the truth of the statement. For Aida, the grass was always greener somewhere else. I could promise her, if she'd seen what I had, she'd be happy to just see the present. I felt that Phoenix had the best deal out of the three of us—seeing what had once happened felt less intense. You couldn't change it, or worry about it, because it had already happened.

"What are the other incubi like?" I asked, changing the subject.

Aida smirked, rolling her eyes. "Seriously hot. It was insane—it looked like I'd stepped into a photoshoot. I felt sorry for them though, especially Kristos's brother. He wanted to wait to hear from Draven, but his father just wouldn't listen. I hope he doesn't suffer because of it," she replied, looking downcast. "And that poor Druid who was being tortured. The Destroyers are horrific."

"Tell me about it," I replied with a shudder. "I just hope you never have to see Azazel. He was…something else."

"Snakes," Aida replied, her mouth twisted in distaste. "I've never liked snakes."

Field shook his head, doing his best to hide a smirk.

"What?" Aida asked.

"Nothing," he replied innocently.

"No, go on, what's so funny about me hating snakes?" Aida asked testily.

Field laughed, rubbing the back of his neck as we all looked at him. "I was just remembering the time Blue caught one in the forest, and kept it as a pet." I glanced over at Aida—I couldn't remember this happening, but my friend had started to blush furiously.

"Then it escaped," Field continued, "and you marched around The Shade for a week carrying a slingshot and a dagger that your parents didn't know about—you were about nine."

Jovi burst out laughing. "I remember that. You got in so much trouble."

"Yeah, well," Aida retorted. "Snakes are dangerous."

"It was a grass snake, Aida," Field replied dryly.

"Whatever."

I bit my lip, trying not to laugh.

Field suddenly shot up in the air, circling us a few times before flying off up over the house.

"What's his deal?" Jovi asked, amused. I shrugged. I didn't really know Field that well, but sometimes I got the impression with the Hawk boys that they just needed to fly—get up in the air and away from everything. I could relate to that. If I had wings, I didn't think I'd stay long on the ground at any given time.

"He's gone off to think," Aida replied, slumping back on the grass. "He always does that when there's something on his mind."

Jovi nodded, dismissing Field's departure. I looked over at him, noticing how the sunlight made his hair look more brown than black. His stubble was quickly appearing after his clean-shaven appearance for Sherus and Nuriya's party.

While I was studying him, the image of him being impaled on the spear suddenly flashed into my mind, and I looked away quickly.

"Are you okay?" Aida asked with concern.

"Yeah, I'm fine. Just thinking about the Nevertide Oracle," I replied, half-truthfully.

"Do you think she was trying to warn you of the Destroyers coming?" she asked.

I nodded. I did—the panic in her eyes as I ran toward her had been all too apparent.

"I guess we can assume she's on our side, then," Aida concluded. "It was probably true what Draven told us—that passing on the gift had been done kindly. She obviously didn't know about Azazel at the time."

"I think you're right," I agreed. "I think in the bathroom she was trying to warn me as well. Not about Draven, but Azazel."

"So that's it?" Jovi interrupted. "You're just going to trust Draven now?"

I looked over at Aida, who shrugged.

"What else can we do?" she asked. "He's the only one who has any answers, and the only one who can help us understand what we're seeing—even if he does have his own motives, we still need him."

Jovi grunted in disapproval, but didn't argue with his sister.

I stared up at the aqua-blue sky, trying to remove the visions from my mind. The Druid had mentioned another training session tomorrow, and I was dreading it. I didn't think I could handle much more—how could I handle seeing more of my friends getting into danger? How was I supposed to behave day-to-day when I had seen Jovi's death? I would feel cut off from others, always on the periphery, looking in … crushingly alone.

"I still think we should try to get out of here," Jovi remarked idly, looking toward the far end of the garden.

"No!" I retorted, more passionately than I should have.

Both Aida and Jovi stared at me.

"Sorry, it's just, we shouldn't. It's dangerous. Don't even think of doing something like that till we have a plan," I emphasized, pulling awkwardly at the overgrown grass.

"I won't," Jovi replied gently. "Don't worry, Vita, we're going to be okay."

"I know," I murmured, "sorry."

Jovi looked at me with deep concern, and I stood up, wanting to go and lie down. If I said anything more, I was worried that the truth would come tumbling out, and it just wasn't the right time to say anything.

"I'm going inside, the sun's giving me a headache."

Aida nodded, looking up at me from the grass.

"Do you want company?" she asked.

I shook my head. "I'm fine. I'll come back down in a bit."

I walked toward the greenhouse without looking back.

SERENA
[HAZEL AND TEJUS'S DAUGHTER]

Using True Sight, I made sure that Draven and Bijarki were out of earshot and then turned to my brother, who was still warming himself by the fire.

"So the woman you saw—the diary must belong to her, right?" I asked.

"Yeah. I even saw her diary—the kid, Draven, ran through the house with it." He looked contemplative, and kind of sad.

"Was there anything else?" I asked.

Phoenix frowned. "In the first vision I had of the

Oracle—like I mentioned to Draven—there were other servants around, and they appeared to be human, which is odd. Why would they have bothered bringing humans to the In-Between? And what happened to them?"

I frowned too, shrugging. The fact was this whole house had a human 1800s feel—from the architecture to the furniture. Almost like it had been... transplanted here.

"Anyway," Phoenix went on, "in the vision with the diary, the Oracle, Almus and Draven just seemed happy. I want to know what happened to *her*—have you got any further with the diary?"

"No, not yet, I haven't really had time. I'll read more today. I'm just hoping she'll provide answers on how she regained her sight...I couldn't imagine that happening to any of you."

"Don't worry," my brother replied, trying to smile. "No signs of that happening yet."

Not yet.

But it didn't mean it wouldn't. I doubted if Phoenix would even want to tell me if it did start happening. No doubt he would try to protect me from that too, like everything else.

"And what about the tree?" I asked. "It was weird that

Draven didn't comment on it. It seems like a strange thing to have a vision about."

"I know," Phoenix replied, concern marring his features. "I don't get that. I'll go and have a look at it later—if it's even still there."

"I'll come with you," I suggested. "We can go together."

"Focus on the diary, Serena. I saw the visions of the Oracle for a reason, and I'm not sure why. She obviously meant a lot to Draven and his father, so I can't imagine they would have deliberately let anything happen to her. Maybe Azazel and his Destroyers somehow managed to get her out of this house."

"You don't believe him about Azazel not being able to see us here?" I asked, surprised. From Aida's vision, I had felt secure that at least the Destroyers definitely didn't know we were here—obviously, they realized we were in Eritopia, but didn't seem to have any other clues as to our whereabouts.

"No, I believe him," Phoenix corrected me. "I'm just saying she was caught *somehow*. If we're going to escape the same fate, I want to know how."

I felt relieved that my brother was starting to trust the Druid. I was certain that I did—to an extent. He was secretive, and I was sure there was a lot he wasn't telling us, but I did believe his intentions were good.

"All right, I'll get on with reading the diary. But I think you should ask Draven again about the tree. Maybe he was just preoccupied with the other stuff. It must have some relevance."

"Maybe," my brother agreed. "By the way, did you warn the other girls about Bijarki?"

"Oh, no—not yet. I forgot. There's been so much going on," I replied, mentally kicking myself for still not mentioning it. It wasn't Aida I was worried about though—she was more than capable of handling herself. It was Vita I had concern for.

"You should. He can't keep his eyes off Vita. If Draven needed to warn him away from them, then you need to alert the girls."

"I know," I replied. "I'll tell them. Do you think he means any harm though?"

Phoenix shook his head. "Not harm exactly, I just don't think he can stop himself. It's his nature, right?"

"Right."

I wished I knew more about the incubus species. It was all well and good warning Vita about him, but we were sharing a house with the incubus for the foreseeable future, and so it would have been helpful to know exactly what to warn her *of.* As far as I could tell at the moment, he just seemed to radiate a particular type of charm, and with his good looks, it could be overwhelming. Even I couldn't help but be hyper-aware of his presence physically. I had met a couple of nymphs when I'd visited Ruby and Ash in Nevertide, and noticed the overwhelming attraction that was totally hypnotic when I'd been around them, but the incubus' charms were far subtler…you didn't lose your head or reasoning, but it was like my whole body just seemed to be drawn to him, no matter how many times I shook it off or outright ignored him. The nymphs could be deadly—Ash and Ruby had only kept them in Nevertide after they'd promised not to mess around with the sentries, but even then, it had been a reluctant agreement. I wondered if incubi could be just as deadly.

"Don't worry too much," my brother remarked, noticing me worriedly speculating. "I'm sure he doesn't mean anything by it. Just make them aware."

I nodded, flopping into the vacated chair.

"I miss home," I sighed. The heat was instantly unbearable by the fire, but I felt too drained to move. "Do you think Mom and Dad are okay?"

"I guess so," Phoenix replied quietly. "They don't know we're missing. So I'm assuming that they're fine."

"But how can they not *know*? We're their children...I mean, they must somehow be able to tell. Feel that something's missing, at least? How can we be completely eradicated from our homes, The Shade?" I still couldn't get my head around the concept that we could be missing from The Shade and have no one notice our absence.

"Obviously, these Daughters are powerful—I can't understand how else they'd manage to fool jinn and witches. The only thing that makes me a bit hopeful about the whole thing is that the Nevertide Oracle managed to break the magic somehow, so there *is* a way."

"Yeah, if you're an Ancient," I groaned. "It's not like there are any of them about anymore." *And even if there were, they'd be the last creatures I'd ask for help.*

"Which is why we need to rescue the Oracle," Phoenix replied firmly. "I've been thinking about it, and it seems to be the only way we can get out of here. It also fits in with the Druid's plans about making sure Azazel is robbed of that power...I'm hoping he'll agree to it, and help us."

"Slight drawback is that we can't actually leave the

house," I replied.

"But we do. Vita saw it. It's the only way."

I wasn't so sure about that. Whatever Vita had seen must have been terrifying for her to hold back telling us everything.

"Maybe," I conceded slowly. "But we need a proper plan. I'm not going tearing off into the jungle again. It would be suicide."

"We'll make a plan," Phoenix reassured me. "We won't do anything stupid. But I'm sick of waiting around in this house. I'm fine to have a few more sessions on how to access our visions, but after that, we need to take action. We'll get home somehow, Serena, I promise you that."

I smiled at my brother, knowing he was trying to make me feel better. He was always so determined, like he could bend the whole world to his will. He was a bit like Jovi in that respect—both totally optimistic that they could fight and overcome whatever obstacles were thrown our way. It didn't matter that I didn't believe him, and I wasn't even sure if he entirely believed himself.

"Okay, I'm going to read. Speak to Draven about the tree, okay?"

Phoenix nodded, looking out of the window.

"Don't worry, I will."

Aida

After Vita went off to lie down, my brother left me dozing in the grass—after telling me about a million times not to go anywhere near the edge of the boundary.

Yeah, right.

Like I'd do that by myself in a million years. I wasn't stupid. I knew what lay in wait for us outside of the house's protection, perhaps better than he did. I was perfectly content lying in the sunshine now that it was past its midday blaze. Plus, thanks to the Druid's unhealthy obsession with fire, the house managed to get hotter than it did out here. I'd moved over to the shade of a tree so my skin didn't burn and peel, wishing I had my phone to listen to music—or a book, a magazine, or *anything* to take my mind off the visions. The house was full of books, but I didn't figure they'd have anything that would hold my interest, even if I did manage to find something in English. Sadly, it looked like it would be just me and my whirring head, trying to battle off the feeling of the damp tunnels, the cries of that tortured Druid and the downcast, disappointed face of the incubus. And the Destroyer. I wouldn't be forgetting those black eyes in a hurry, nor its snarling, hissing voice.

I had just managed to doze off when I heard the familiar sound of wings flapping overhead. I opened my eyes, shielding them from the sun with my hand, and squinted at Field, watching him land softly in the grass next to me.

"Hey," he said, greeting me.

There was a *lot* running through my mind, so it was a testament to the effect Field had on me that all my thoughts switched entirely to him. I sat up quickly, feeling awkward.

"Hey," I replied, as casually as I could.

"Mind if I sit?" he asked.

Unable to trust myself to talk, I shifted over so that we could share the shade. Never in my life had Field asked to sit with me—not once. It wasn't that I was bitter about it or anything, but the request took me by surprise. He sat down, close enough that I could smell his skin—a mixture of smoke from the fires that roared in the house, and the fresh smell of outdoors. He kept his aquamarine eyes on the house, and I was grateful that I didn't have to meet his gaze. I always felt with Field that if he looked close enough, all my feelings would be laid bare for him to see.

"What's up?" I asked, looking at the ground.

"I wanted to apologize for the snake thing earlier," he replied, his voice going down a notch. "I know that the Destroyers are nothing like that—I shouldn't have made light of it. Sorry."

"What?" I replied, genuinely aghast. "I really wasn't offended—it was just a joke. I'd forgotten that had even happened."

"Yeah, it was a long time ago," he replied. When I glanced up at him, I could see that his hand was resting on the back of his neck, a sign that he felt awkward. I had actually been referring to the joke, not the original event with the snake, which, come to think of it, I was kind of amazed that he could remember something so irrelevant that far back.

"You have a good memory," I replied, clearing my throat.

"Yeah."

He sighed a moment later. "Maura panicked as well. She made me check under the bed and in all the wardrobes. You weren't alone."

Of course he remembered because of Maura—idiot.

"Right," I replied, suddenly wishing for the conversation to end. I wasn't sure if he was bringing up Maura because he wanted to talk about it—but why would he speak to me anyway? I remembered that no one was supposed to know they had broken up. Serena had told me that she'd overheard the conversation. It would be inappropriate and downright weird for me to say anything.

"Are you okay though, after the visions?" he asked, unexpectedly turning to stare at me.

"Um, yeah," I replied, kind of dazed. I wasn't used to having Field's full attention. I looked toward the house, hoping that someone would emerge from it—I was even willing for it to be the Druid or Bijarki. A conversation with them would be less awkward for me than this one.

"It sounded intense, the torture vision," he clarified. "I wouldn't want you—any of you—to think that you couldn't talk about it, share the burden. It must be tough, seeing someone else's pain that way. Knowing you can't do anything to help."

I nodded. Field had hit the nail on the head. That had been the most difficult thing with both the incubus and the tortured Druid. How helpless I'd felt just watching, knowing that we were the cause of both those incidents, in a way. If Draven didn't insist on keeping us hidden here, perhaps we'd be able to provide the remaining incubi with hope, and if the Destroyers knew where we were, they wouldn't be torturing someone for the information.

"I was terrified. Even if I hadn't just been watching, and unable to do anything, I doubt that I would have been brave enough to stop it. You hear all these stories about our parents doing these amazing things, sacrificing themselves to help a loved one or an innocent…but if it came down to it"—I hesitated—"I don't know if I could do what they've done."

"You don't know that," Field replied softly. "No one knows what they're capable of until it actually happens. And our parents have made mistakes. We all do, it's part of being human." He smiled then, correcting himself. "Well, supernatural, but still human on the inside, despite our abilities."

"I guess," I replied, not entirely convinced. I thought that deep down you always knew what you were capable of—what kind of person you were. I knew that I could act tough, and train with the rest of GASP's members with confidence, not afraid of a few bruises or on one occasion, thanks to Phoenix, a cracked rib, but I didn't seem to have that steely metal inside me that I saw in my dad, my mom, my kickass grandparents Vivienne and Xavier, Tejus, Derek, Sofia, Ben, Rose…the list went on.

Jovi appeared from the smashed doorway of the greenhouse and made his way across the garden. His hair was slicked back and wet—he'd obviously just had a shower, and I suddenly found myself longing for cold jets of water and some fresh clothes. The first was thankfully possible—the latter not so much.

"You're going to get burnt, Aida," he said as he approached. My skin wasn't as naturally tan as Jovi's, so I was more susceptible to being burnt.

"I was in the shade," I replied, pushing my fingers into my arm to see if I'd caught the sun. They left marks. Oops. Perhaps I had overstayed my welcome out here. I wondered if Draven would have some kind of herb around, like lavender, that Vita could turn into a paste for me.

Field rose to his feet, offering an arm to help me up. Trying not to blush, I took it, allowing him to pull me up, but making sure that he didn't have to take my full body weight.

Get a grip, girl.

I really needed to start having some stern words with myself about my general levels of confidence around guys. It was fine when I was going through puberty, it was kind of the norm, but now it was just getting ridiculous.

As my hand came into contact with Field's, my whole body felt like it had been electrified. I dropped it as instantly as I stood up, surreptitiously rubbing my palm on my sweatpants to try to shake the feeling away.

"I was thinking we should continue our training sessions while we're here," Jovi was saying to Field. "At some point, hopefully sooner rather than later, we're going to leave this house—and I want us to be ready for whatever we face when we do."

"Good point," Field agreed, glancing over at me. "We should all do it. Oracles included."

"Of course," I replied, privately wondering how I would have the energy. The visions had taken a lot out of me—

not just physically, but mentally too. I only hoped they would get easier as time went on.

"See you both later," I added, moving toward the house. I'd had enough of weird feelings for one day—first the visions and now with Field. I was done in. I didn't want to feel anything, and the only way to accomplish that in this place would be to take the world's longest nap.

Serena

After speaking with my brother, I went back upstairs to read more of Elissa's diary. The house was still and quiet, but I could hear the muffled conversation of Aida, Jovi, and Field outside. I looked in our room, checking to see if Vita was okay, thinking it would be a good time to talk about Bijarki, but she was fast asleep. I let her rest. After what the three of them had been through today, I wasn't surprised that she was exhausted.

I grabbed the diary from the night-stand, and went through to the spare room where I'd originally found it. It felt right to be reading it in what I assumed had been the

Oracle's bedroom, surrounded by her things, able to get a better sense of her not just as an Oracle but as any other woman—with hopes, dreams and, clearly, a developing relationship with Draven's father.

I opened up the diary where I'd left off, settling myself onto the musty bed. The entry was a few weeks after the last—the Oracle clearly wasn't a regular writer, but perhaps that was a good thing, as long as she had documented what was important.

I had a vision today. It was beautiful. I never wanted it to end. It was of the three of us, Almus and Draven and I, traveling to the eastern city. Draven was much older, in his twenties, I suppose, and we journeyed through the land without fear of Azazel and his Destroyers.

How such an existence became possible, I do not know, but I saw it, so somehow it is a future that could be brought into being. With all my heart, I hope it is how my story unfolds, but I worry that it will not end this way. Tonight, at dinner, Almus spoke of rumors of the Destroyers laying siege to the western citadel. The Druids there have so far been the only ones to hold out against Azazel's rule, but Almus suspects that soon they will fold.

After dinner, Almus escorted me to my room and bade me

goodnight. He hesitated—I am sure of it—at the door, but then did nothing but give me a chaste kiss on the cheek. Still, it was enough to make my insides melt. How embarrassed I am about the feelings I have for him! Why on earth would he wish to begin a relationship with me? I am only a woman in looks, not in physical function. If I can't bear him a child, then what good am I?

I stopped reading, realizing that the Oracle was referring to her reproductive organs—something those twins hadn't had, though I wasn't sure about the Nevertide Oracle. No one in my family had mentioned anything about it, and I hadn't taken much interest. But I had known that Oracles never reproduced…perhaps that was why she'd passed on her gift to my friends and brother. I wondered if she had wanted to leave a part of herself in this world, something that would continue after her eventual death.

I felt sorry for Elissa. It must have been hard to fall in love with a man, knowing that it would be impossible for it to be a real relationship, in the biblical sense of the word. I returned to the diary, skim-reading the next few pages. They were mainly observations about the house, the changing seasons and what she did to occupy her time— mainly reading old history books, sewing and trying to overcome her growing distaste for eating the same food, day in, day out. I could relate to that.

The next entry was about a year apart from the last. The writing was more frantic, the letters spiked and ink blots staining the page.

I had an argument with Almus. He wants to join the rebel forces that are rising up against Azazel. It's a huge mistake. I've been having visions of the bloody battle for weeks, but without seeing its conclusion. I can't be sure that Almus will survive it, and so I am opposed. He tells me he wants a better life for both me and Draven, not stuck in this house forever, but if we were to stay here forever, as long as the three of us were together, I would be happy.

I put the diary down. It made interesting reading, but I desperately wanted to know how the Oracle had avoided blindness, and so far, that hadn't been mentioned, nor any real information on the side-effects of her visions. I also knew the end of the tale—Almus had died protecting the next Oracle who came to visit them—the Nevertide Oracle, whose real name I still didn't know. If he did go and fight in the battle against Azazel before that, he had clearly survived. I wondered if it would be easier speaking to Draven about the battle, and how the Oracle overcame some of her difficulties. He was willing to help with the training, and so I didn't see why he'd have a problem with divulging some of Elissa's secrets.

I left the room, careful to replace the diary in the drawer first.

Still hearing the murmurs of conversation floating from the rooms' open windows as I strode purposefully along the corridor and then descended the staircase, I hesitated before going to hunt for the Druid. I would have preferred to spend some time with my friends, to put the mysteries aside for a moment, and pretend that everything was normal for a few hours.

It was Draven himself who stopped me. As I reached the ground floor, making my way toward the greenhouse, he emerged from his room, hair sleep-rumpled and his clothes disheveled.

"Can I help you?" he asked, yawning.

Instantly, I was put in a bad mood. It hardly seemed like the right time for a *nap*. Rationally I knew it was the heat that was making everyone drowsy, including myself, but I felt that the Druid, as our sole protector here, should be putting a bit more effort into helping us—making plans as to what we might do next.

"Did I wake you?" I asked, sarcasm coloring my tone. He raised an eyebrow, a smirk appearing on his irritatingly handsome features. He looked lazy and mocking, and I couldn't help thinking of the last time I'd seen him in bed, peaceful and serene, with his tanned muscular torso looking pale in the moonlight.

"I had some questions," I continued hastily, shoving the thoughts aside and getting down to business. "About the Oracle my brother saw living here. When and how did she recover from her blindness?"

"I was not there to witness it, but Elissa regained her sight when she, along with the house, was moved by the Daughters from Earth to Eritopia to create a sanctuary—"

"Whoa, the Daughters moved this entire house from *Earth?*" I interrupted. *That would explain a lot.*

"Indeed," Draven replied. "Elissa had fled to Earth to escape Azazel a couple of hundred years ago, around the time he began capturing Oracles. She cast a spell over herself like a mask so she could hide the shadows on her skin, and took up residence on a plantation where she worked as a servant."

To my annoyance, he paused. "Please, go on," I pressed.

He sighed. "My father at the time, being acutely opposed

to Azazel and needing to do everything he could to stop him collecting more Oracles, managed to track down Elissa's location and convince the Daughters to help create a sanctuary. They scooped up the whole house and planted it here—after expelling the human residents…"

"Expelling the humans?" I couldn't help but interject.

Draven shrugged.

"You saw no reason to ask the Daughters, I guess," I mumbled.

"Of course my father didn't. Asking them questions is always a mistake—the wrong one angers them, and the right one doesn't gain you much of an answer."

I frowned. From where I was standing, it seemed like these Daughters had been pretty generous—helping protect Elissa from Azazel, along with the Druid and his father, and giving her the gift of sight. I wasn't sure why the Druid spoke about them in such negative terms.

"They don't seem that bad," I muttered.

"Because you haven't met them," he countered. "Why do you insist on disagreeing with everything that I tell you? I'm not lying, Serena. I'm telling you this for your own good—the Daughters, should you ever come across them, are…*difficult*, to say the least."

"It's not that I disagree," I replied heatedly, "It's just that you don't tell us anything—or so little that we're always in the dark, and it feels like you do it on purpose."

"That's not the case," Draven replied, far calmer than I was. He reached up, absent-mindedly ruffling the back of his hair. "There's so much about this land—about Eritopia, Azazel, everything—that you don't understand, that you couldn't *hope* to understand. I'm trying to make this as easy on you as I can."

I clenched my jaw in frustration. Every time I thought we were making a bit of a breakthrough in understanding, the answers were instantly blocked off. We had the future and the past to contend with as well, thanks to the visions and the diary, which seemed to make everything more complicated—not clearer, as I had hoped.

"Can you tell me what happened to Elissa, the Oracle?" I asked, folding my arms.

"It's a long story." He sighed.

"I've got the time."

"I haven't. And it's not something I wish to discuss."

His face darkened suddenly, his eyes dimming. Perhaps I was overstepping the mark by demanding answers on Elissa. From what I had read, and from Phoenix's description of the cozy family life they'd led, at least temporarily, it sounded like for all intents and purposes, Elissa had been a mother figure to the Druid. I suspected that it might have been painful for him to discuss her, and, unless I wanted to invoke his anger, it was probably better to stay silent on the subject—at least for now.

"Fine," I retorted, backing away from him, moving toward the greenhouse.

"There was one thing," Draven replied before I left. "Clothing. I noticed you could all use extra items—there should be some upstairs in the attic from the previous owners. You can access it through the hallway opposite the werewolf's room."

"Oh, okay. Thanks."

I was taken aback by the offer. It seemed such a *human* thing to suggest—and considerate. I doubted there would be much up there that hadn't been eaten by moths and disintegrated, but the offer was kind nevertheless.

"I'll tell the others," I added.

"And you *can* start calling me by my name, Draven. I've heard some of you still referring to me as 'the Druid', which I've begun to find mildly irritating."

I wanted to laugh at that—he'd just this second referred

to Jovi as 'the werewolf.'

"Okay," I replied, "*Draven*. And the werewolf's Jovi, by the way."

"I know."

I shrugged, leaving him standing in the hallway. So, it looked like we were on first-name terms now...I wondered if *that* was the way to get the answers we needed: to start treating the Druid—*Draven*, I corrected—as a friend and ally, rather than our enemy. He didn't exactly make it easy by being so shut off every waking hour, but with a little time, and a little patience, perhaps we could wear him down.

Vita

I had slept for ages, and when I woke up it was dusk outside. Aida was fast asleep next to me in the bed, her limbs sprawled out across the mattress. I felt groggy, in need of cold water and yet another shower. I wondered where Serena was, but figured she'd be off somewhere reading the diary or with Jovi and the rest of the boys.

Realizing I was starving thanks to a loud rumble coming from my stomach, I showered quickly and changed back into my pajamas. I decided to wake Aida. I didn't want her to miss out on dinner, partly because she'd need it, and partly because all our lives would be a nightmare if she went without food, and she'd be the first to admit it.

"Aida?" I shook her awake.

"Eugh," she groaned, wiping the sleep from her eyes. "What time is it?"

"Evening. Dinner time, hopefully."

"I'm starving," she replied, sitting upright on the bed and swiftly moving off to go and get herself freshened up. "Have you seen the others yet?" she asked at the bathroom doorway.

"No. I guess they're downstairs somewhere. I'll wait for you."

"Thanks. I'll be quick."

She shut the door and I heard the sounds of the shower running. I stuck my head out of the window, enjoying the slightly cooler evening air on my face.

A couple of minutes later, we both headed downstairs, making a beeline for the dining room. Serena was hovering outside the doorway.

"Serena?" I asked, wondering what she was doing.

A look of relief passed her face.

"It's just Bijarki and Draven in there. I didn't want to go in alone," she replied, laughing at her trepidation. I didn't blame her. I would have done the same in her position, though it surprised me that Serena felt the same way. Normally she was bold—sometimes too bold. It wasn't like her.

"Come on," Aida instructed. "I'm starving. We can make awkward conversation till the boys get here—are they still upstairs?"

"I think so." Serena nodded. "They're not outside."

Aida pushed the door open. The Druid and Bijarki had obviously been deep in hushed conversation, but when we entered, they both closed their mouths. Bijarki rose to his feet, moving the chair next to him back from the table and gesturing for me to sit down.

"Bijarki," the Druid bit out. It was a warning, and I moved around to the opposite side of the table, pretending I hadn't seen the proffered chair. Aida and Serena sat on either side of me, Serena closest to the Druid, and Aida closest to the door.

"What have we got tonight?" Serena asked as a joke, lifting the warming plate to reveal the same meal we'd had every night since we'd arrived.

The Druid semi-smiled, drinking from his glass.

"You'll get used to it," he replied dryly. I looked over at his place setting. As usual, there was nothing there. It struck me as very odd that we hadn't seen him eat once since we'd arrived. It wasn't like he was wasting away—his broad form must have needed some sustenance, and the idea that he chose not to eat in front of us unnerved me. Serena glanced over at his absence of food.

"Not eating again?" she asked.

"I've already—"

"You've already eaten, right," she replied, finishing the Druid's sentence with a frustrated sigh. "Another mystery that you won't give us an answer to."

"Did you speak to your friends about the clothing?" the Druid replied, ignoring her comment.

"Oh, no." Serena turned to us with an apologetic shrug. "There are more clothes in the attic, if either of you want them."

"That would be good," Aida replied, pulling at her tank top. "Be nice to wear something other than pajamas for a change."

The door opened, and Jovi, Phoenix and Field walked in. They all had damp hair, dripping onto their evening shirts. They smiled in our direction and nodded a silent greeting to the Druid and Bijarki. Jovi took a seat next to the incubus, both of them clearly uncomfortable with the arrangement.

"We wanted to know if you'd made any plans," Field began, directing his question at the Druid. "What will happen once they're adequately trained as Oracles? Are we waiting for a vision to tell us what to do?"

"We are waiting for a vision, yes. Until then, there's not a lot we can do," Draven replied. He glanced over at Serena, as if expecting her to argue with him, but she remained quiet.

"What about the incubi?" Field countered. "Can't they be of some help, if there's an entire army ready to bring down Azazel?"

"It wasn't exactly a big army," Aida added. "I can't see them making much of a difference."

"We can't rely on the incubi," Bijarki interjected before Draven could reply. "Most of them, and no doubt some of the remaining force that Aida saw in her vision, are already aligned with Azazel. They can't be trusted. Too many families have been torn apart by him and the Destroyers. Some family members joined him willingly, while others vowed to fight against him—but then, of course, blood proved to be thicker than water, making many incubi in the army turn traitor to help family members who were already under Azazel's rule. Kristos and I were betrayed by someone—we were sure of it."

"And what about your family members?" Serena asked.

"Already lost to me."

Silence fell over the table, with only the sound of cutlery scraping against the plates. I looked down, busying myself with eating until someone changed the conversation. After a while, I could feel Bijarki watching me. I put down my knife and fork, appetite gone. When I looked up, his gaze was swiftly averted, but I noticed that the Druid was frowning at him. Another warning.

"There must be some," Field continued awkwardly. "Some incubi who would be ready to fight if need be. What about the chief or leader's son Aida saw in her vision? He seemed willing to wait for you." He turned to Draven. "He obviously trusts that you'll come through for them."

"He's Kristos's brother," Bijarki replied quietly. "Sverik. He was meant to join us on the mission, but his father found out his plan and forbade it. Sverik was always the favorite son—and their father, Arid, wouldn't let him join us on such a dangerous mission. And as you heard, he doesn't trust Draven either. I believe the traitor was in his ranks—perhaps even Arid himself, though I'm not sure what he would stand to gain."

"But what about Sverik—can't we somehow get a message to him directly? If they march on Azazel, they're going to die, right?" Aida looked distraught. It took me by surprise how much the incubus in the vision had moved her with his plight and garnered her empathy. Bijarki looked over at Draven, waiting for him to respond.

The Druid was silent for a few moments, staring into his empty glass.

"Perhaps we can contact him," he replied eventually. "But we would need to be careful. Is it something you'd be willing to do?" Draven directed his question at the incubus, who nodded.

"I owe it to Kristos."

"Then we will find a way," agreed Draven.

"What about the others?" Aida asked earnestly. "Are there any that we can trust?"

Bijarki looked doubtful, and seemed to be contemplating his answer when a strange thing happened. As soon as my gaze settled on him, waiting for what he would say, he looked up at me, his eyes alight, as if I was the only person in the whole world he wanted to see in that moment.

"Bijarki!" Draven snapped at him. The incubus shook his

head, turning his attention back to Aida.

"What were you saying?" he asked politely.

Aida, Serena and I looked at one another in confusion. The boys had been sitting on his side of the table, and so hadn't seen the sudden change come over the incubus. Instead, they were looking at Draven, not understanding where the sudden outburst had come from.

"I was asking if it would be safe to inform any of the other incubi that we're here, that there might be hope?" Aida repeated herself slowly.

"I don't think so," Bijarki replied, focused again, as if the last few moments hadn't happened at all. "It's too risky. I don't know who is loyal to Arid and who is loyal to Sverik. I've been away too long, and none of them will trust me, especially when they find out about Kristos's death."

"Are there other creatures we can trust who might be able to help?" Jovi asked. "I mean, besides the Druids and the incubi, what other supernaturals are here? Not counting the shape-shifters, of course," he added. I felt Serena shudder slightly at the reference to the creatures she'd followed into the swamp. I had only heard the account second-hand, but even that had been enough to freak me out and make me dread what other inhabitants Eritopia might contain.

"Many," the Druid replied curtly, "but none that you'd wish to know, trust me. Not on this star, anyway. There are others elsewhere in Eritopia's galaxy—the Deargs, the Sluaghs, the Kelpie, Lamias…and many more that you wouldn't wish to know."

I'd heard of none of these creatures, and I doubt any other GASP members had either.

"And the storm hounds?" Serena asked. "We saw them on a map, marked near the house. I take it they're as deadly as they sound?"

"Actually, no," Draven replied with a smile. "The storm hounds were harmless—and useful. They were attuned to evil thoughts and deeds. When the Destroyers approached the area, the storm hounds would give warning."

"You said 'were'; what happened to them?" I asked.

"The Destroyers hunted them to extinction. They didn't appreciate the hounds providing a warning whenever they approached."

It sounded like none of the supernatural species were free from Azazel's tyranny. Once again, I started to feel a small bubble of anxiety press on my chest. If Azazel could kill and destroy so many, then what chance did we have against him—especially when he could see us coming through the visions of the Oracle?

"What does he want?" Field asked Draven. "Azazel, I mean. It seems like he's bent on destroying everything. What's his goal?"

"Power," Draven replied simply.

All of us kept our gaze on the Druid, waiting for him to elaborate. The whole room was silent for a few moments, and you could have heard a pin drop. Then, with what seemed like a great deal of reluctance, Draven spoke.

"The Druids were originally a peaceful people. We lived within our citadels, each clan specializing in certain knowledge and influence. There were the lawmakers, those who kept the peace, the book keepers who guarded our sacred texts, the botanists who kept the magic of nature, and the philosophers, who were the highest-ranking of all the Druids, combining the knowledge of all four disciplines. There were six leading philosophers—my father was one, and Azazel was another.

"From the start—according to my father, of course; I was not even born when he was elevated to position of philosopher—Azazel failed to see the benefits of the democratic system that the Druids adhered to. He was greedy for absolute power, frequently enraged by the fact that the philosophers gave the other disciplines such a free rein. Letting them rule themselves, in a sense, with little intervention. Azazel must have realized at some point how much power he could wield throughout Eritopia if only the other philosophers were removed from their position and it was he alone who commanded the citadels.

"His first move was to slaughter the rest of the philosophers. A few, like my father, managed to get away. But they went into hiding." At this, Draven curled his lip into a sneer. I wondered why he disagreed with them running and hiding. Wasn't he doing exactly the same thing now?

"Azazel was free to rule the citadels. With the help of an Oracle, one long dead now, he managed to make his power absolute. There was uprising after uprising—whether he expected this or not, I do not know. But he slaughtered freely. So much blood was spilt in those first years."

"But what about the Destroyers?" Serena asked after a pause. "Where does that species come from?"

Draven smirked, but his eyes were deeply pained, tightening at the corners, as if he was recalling a distinctly painful and distasteful memory.

"The Destroyers are Druids. Those who joined Azazel

rather than fight against him."

"What?" Serena retorted, echoing my own thoughts. "But they're half snake, right? How can that happen?"

"They are," Draven replied softly.

Serena opened her mouth to speak again, unsatisfied, as we all were, at his answer.

"That's enough," Draven replied. "Enough for tonight. I need to leave. Training will commence tomorrow morning again." He stood up, and abruptly left the table. I glanced toward Bijarki, and met his stare head on. His eyes were bright again, and I got the distinct impression that he'd been watching me for a long time, but I'd been too engrossed in the Druid's story to notice. It was unnerving.

What is his deal?

"Bijarki, I wish to speak with you," Draven called from the door.

The incubus stood up from his chair and, giving a small bow in the direction of Serena, Aida and me, wished us a good night.

SERENA

We all left the dinner table and walked upstairs to our bedrooms. I was in a complete daze, mulling over the Druid's story. The havoc that Azazel had wreaked on Eritopia was clearly severe, but I felt that now I had more questions than answers. What struck me as strange was the lack of involvement of the Daughters. Weren't they supposed to be protectors of the stars within the Eritopia region? Where had they been while all this was going on? And, if the Druids had known of an Oracle before Azazel's uprising, why had they not seen that it was coming, done more to stop it? What confused me the most was the question that had gone unanswered—how had the Druids become half serpent? Was it some dark magic at play here, that they had become so evil and corrupted that they had taken on the form of such a creature? I shivered despite the still-humid heat that permeated the house. I would not sleep well tonight.

We parted at the top of the staircase, the boys going one way and us following Aida on to our room. None of us spoke. I guessed we were all reeling from the information that Draven had just imparted.

Another question I had was how the incubi fit into all of this. Had they lived peacefully with the Druids before Azazel's uprising? To be honest, it did seem strange to me that two such different species would occupy the same space in harmony—it wasn't GASP's experience that such coexistence was easy, except for in The Shade, of course.

I turned to Vita, recalling the conversation we needed to have about the incubus. Tonight, he had acted particularly strangely, his eyes fixed on Vita as if she were something he wished to devour. It was worrying, more so because occasionally I felt that Vita almost succumbed to his spell…but perhaps I was wrong.

"I left out some of the conversation I overheard between

Bijarki and the Druid when I went with Jovi and Field to spy on them," I began once we were safely in the room with the door shut. "Draven warned Bijarki away from us in a way that made me think that we—or you, in particular—need to be wary of him. I just don't trust him."

Vita blushed furiously, looking embarrassed.

"Of course I will. I'm not interested, obviously," she muttered.

Worried that I'd hurt her feelings, I blundered on. "It's just that we don't know much about them as a species. And what we do know, or what the myths say, well… it's not great."

Aida started laughing, collapsing back on the bed.

"If Bijarki's attentions were on me the way they are on Vita, I doubt I'd be able to hold back. The guy's *smoking* hot."

"And a weirdo," I retorted, rolling my eyes.

"He's not a weirdo," Aida replied. "He's a cutie-pie. And has good taste." She leered at Vita, and then fell about snorting again.

"Seriously? Anyway, you're talking crap, you've only ever had eyes for Field—so you can stop pretending anyone else has a chance," I said, smiling smugly as her eyes narrowed in my direction.

"Honestly, Serena," Vita replied, smiling at last, "I'm fine. He does make me nervous, but I can hold my own. He'll get bored soon anyway."

"Okay," I replied uncertainly. I didn't believe that. I'd seen the way the incubus had looked at her—like she was his birthday and Christmas present rolled into one. He wasn't going to get over that crush, or whatever it was, anytime soon. I made another vow that I would start researching incubi as soon as I could—there were thousands of books scattered about this place, one of them must contain some information on the species, even if it was just a few references in the history books of Eritopia.

* * *

Sleep didn't come. The air was too hot, and I kept going over Draven's story in my mind, trying to make sense of it all. It must have been around midnight when I gave up trying to rest and decided that I would have a better chance of dropping off reading something—namely, Elissa's diary.

I picked up the still-lit lamp, and carried it out into the corridor. The house was completely silent, the loudest noise coming from the thumping inside my ribcage as I tried to avert my eyes from the creepy stuffed animals and the hell, fire and brimstone ceiling murals.

Moving swiftly along to Elissa's room, I pushed the door open and, placing the lamp I'd brought with me on the dresser, I lit another in the corner of the room, trying to remove some of the shadows that jutted out on the walls of the room.

Once again, I opened where I'd left off last.

Almus has left. He departed early yesterday morning, saying he would return in a few days. He hopes to find the remaining philosophers he suspects went into hiding in the mountains. He plans to return them here, and plan an attack of their own— aligning with the incubi and the Deargs to bring Azazel down. I can see nothing of his future. It has gone dark where he is concerned. I feel hopeless. Anxiety gnaws at me constantly, and the only thing I am able to do is keep my fears away from Draven as best I can. He is such a sweet boy—he has his father's eyes, and his temperament too. I love him like he was my own child, and hope for his sake more than my own that the vision I had of the three of us crossing a safe path through the jungle to the nearest citadel is one that begins here.

I turned the page, eager to know what came next. Before I could read the first line, I almost jumped out of my skin as the door was pushed open. Draven stood in the doorway, looking mildly amused at the fright he'd just given me.

"You scared the crap out of me," I grumbled.

"Sorry, I—" He stopped mid-sentence, his gaze resting on the leather-bound diary. "Where did you find that?" he asked coldly.

"In the drawer—the dresser," I replied meekly, feeling guilty for snooping around and reading the private thoughts of a woman who, for all intents and purposes, was his mother. He leaned over, taking the book from my hand. I let him, watching as he gently caressed the leather of the notebook.

"I'm sorry," I whispered.

"It's all right," he muttered after a pause.

He handed the book back to me, his gray eyes sorrowful. I placed it beside me, wondering why he had ventured up here in the first place. From his reaction, I didn't think he'd known the diary was still here.

"What happened to her?" I asked again, knowing I was pushing my luck.

"Not tonight, Serena. I've told you enough. Let some ghosts lie."

I stayed silent for once—ignoring the burning need I had

to know more about her, to finally put her to rest.

"I have no doubt that you'll keep reading it," he continued, his voice slightly softer. "You can find out that way."

I nodded, grateful that I would no longer have to hide my reading of it in front of him. If we were going to try to trust one another, then the fewer secrets between us the better. Not that I didn't think the Druid had plenty of his own which he fully intended to keep.

"Did you find the clothes?" he asked, his gaze sweeping over my ridiculous frilly nightgown.

"I'll take them up to the attic tomorrow morning. No way am I going up there in the dark," I muttered.

"The house is perfectly safe," he replied. "It's only outside that you need to be wary."

I wanted to laugh.

"Draven, I'm sorry, but this house is like something out of a horror story. The stuffed animals, the creepy pictures everywhere—just the fact that it's falling to pieces around us would be enough of a red flag on its own, without the rest of it."

"Really?" he replied, his expression curious. "I had never thought of it that way. I suppose you may find it a little odd. I suppose I don't really notice it that much anymore."

I thought about all the years he'd lived here…since the eighteen hundreds. That was an impossible amount of time to remain in one place. How he had not gone completely insane, I would never know.

"You must have been lonely here," I said instead.

He shrugged. "I like my own company, perhaps more than the company of others."

"How do you know that if you've never had company— other than Elissa and your father?" I countered. "Maybe you're lonely and you don't even know it."

"I consider you and your friends company, and I've found you all exceedingly tiresome."

I laughed out loud at his reply, quickly muffling the sound with my sleeve so as not to wake the others. Well, at least he was upfront about some things.

"We're not exactly having the time of our lives here, either," I replied, hoping to remind him that it was *he* who had brought us here—we were not uninvited guests who were overstaying their welcome.

"I know that. Which is why I want you all to be as comfortable as possible. Hence the clothing. And anything else you need, just say. If it is in my power to give it, I will do so."

"I appreciate it," I replied gently. I meant it. I did believe that he was doing what he thought was best for us. No matter how much I disagreed with his methods, I felt there was an honesty behind it all—a reluctance to have Azazel destroy any more lives than he had done already.

"It's late," he replied eventually, moving toward the door. "Please rest. I have a feeling there is much ahead of us."

Before I could ask him what he meant, he had left the room, closing the door firmly behind him. I rose up off the bed. I wasn't going to sleep in here, it was too creepy. I took the diary with me and picked up the lamp, putting the other out. As I crept back along the corridor to my bedroom, I couldn't help thinking of the night in the jungle when he'd come to save me. Amidst all the confusion and panic that night, I could still recall how it felt to be in his arms. How warm his skin had been in comparison to my body temperature. How quick and controlled his stride had been as he carried me across the lawn, like an animal coiled and ready to strike at a moment's notice…

Draven was certainly intriguing.

AIDA

Before breakfast, and far too early for my liking, Serena hauled us out of bed and dragged us along the corridor, trying to find the entrance to the attic that the Druid, or *Draven*, had told her about. The prospect of a change of clothing was appealing, but I dreaded what we'd find in the attic. No doubt it would be moth-eaten rags straight from the eighteenth century. *Great.*

Serena led us to the covered painting at the far end of the hallway. There was no sound from the boys' room, and I suspected they were most likely still fast asleep. Like we should have been.

As we approached the painting, I could see there was another, much smaller, corridor which was shrouded in almost complete darkness. I hadn't noticed it before, but that was understandable—the entry was partially blocked by piles of books, and more paintings that leaned against the wall. The entrance was covered in cobwebs. Clearly no one had been here in a very long time.

"Another treat from the house of horrors," I muttered, knocking away one of the dust-filled webs. My fear of spiders was minor compared to that of snakes, so I felt just about okay dealing with whatever creepy-crawlies would be coming our way.

"Do you think we need a lamp?" Serena asked, peering down the corridor. None of us had moved from the landing. I doubted any of us were particularly keen on going first. Not just because it was creepy, but because this house was falling apart—one wrong step and we might find ourselves falling through the floor.

"Yeah," Vita replied. "I think so… better safe than sorry."

"Give me a second," Serena replied, dashing back to the spare room. A few moments later she reappeared with one of the gas lamps.

"Hopefully the attic will be lighter." Serena tried to sound upbeat.

"Since when are attics light?" I asked, amused at her efforts to make this venture seem more hopeful. "They are literally the cornerstone of every horror movie—dark, creepy and damp. And I can imagine this one will top them all off."

"Well, it's this or pajamas for eternity," she replied primly.

"Is it too late to vote for pajamas for eternity?" Vita asked, only half-joking.

"Come on," Serena instructed, taking the first step along the corridor, gingerly stepping past the piles of books and paintings. She held the lamp low on the floor, making sure that the floorboards weren't completely rotten.

"It looks okay," she called to us.

I sighed, following her. Vita walked behind me, and together we quietly made our way deeper into the gloom. On our right, the walls were made of crumbling plaster, exposing the brickwork beneath them. There were even more books piled up along here, their covers completely obscured by a thick coating of dust. On the left, the wall was in better condition, with lamps, unlit, at various intervals, and doors leading off into other rooms.

"Should we be exploring any of these?" I asked, as Serena marched past them.

"On the way back," she replied. "I don't want either of you getting more freaked out."

"Oh, thanks," I retorted. "We're not completely useless. I'm not actually that freaked out by this, I—" I broke off, giving a short, and embarrassing, squeal of fright as something brushed against my face. It was just another web, and I shoved it away in irritation.

"You were saying?" Serena replied, stifling laughter.

"That this is a dumb idea," I grumbled.

She ignored me, and we kept going until we reached the end of the corridor. The wall was covered in a velvet drape, which fell in folds on the floor. Leaning forward past Serena, I gave the drape a yank, parting it lengthways till the hallway filled with light. I had exposed a large window that looked out onto the front of the house. The glass was dusty and smeared with dirt, but it was a huge relief to stand bathed in the bright rays of the morning sun.

"Who would put a drape against one of these windows?" I asked curiously. It seemed like the strangest thing to do, especially in a house so in desperate need of some natural light.

"Beats me," replied Serena.

She put the lamp down, pushing the drape further off the window, and we all peered out. I had actually never seen the front of the house—I'd been too nervous about accidentally crossing over the boundaries of the garden to do much exploring.

There was a large courtyard outside, directly in the center of which was a small island of grass, surrounded by a dirt track. Blooming magnolia trees grew in the center, sending their petals scattering across the rest of the courtyard. On either side of the track which led up to the front door of the house—I presumed, as the entrance was covered by a shaded porch—there was more overgrown garden: magnolia trees and weeping willows with wild clusters of flowers and weeds. The dirt track led away from the house for a few yards, ending suddenly, the overgrown garden becoming replaced by the swamp land. The effect of a plantation house being lifted from its natural surroundings and dumped in the middle of a jungle was more obvious here than in the back garden. The difference was startlingly pronounced, and for the first time I found myself genuinely believing Draven's tale—it felt like I finally had evidence that such a miraculous thing had taken place.

"Wow," Vita breathed. "This looks so weird."

"Do you think one of those is the magnolia tree that Phoenix saw in his vision?" Serena asked.

"Could be," I replied, "we should tell him."

"I said yesterday that he should go and look for the tree," Serena murmured in reply, "but I don't know if he did or not. He didn't mention it."

I thought that if he'd found the tree in his vision, he would have said something, so I assumed that he hadn't. Turning away from the window, I looked around.

"Where to next?" I asked. There was another door on our left, but that was it. I looked up at the ceiling, but couldn't see any kind of trap door that would indicate an entrance to the attic. Without waiting for the others, I pushed open the door. It groaned loudly from disuse, and then opened up into a small, completely bare room... except for a narrow set of stairs leading upward.

"This must be the way," I said, beckoning the others through. There were two windows in here, unobscured by drapes this time, and sending shafts of light across the bare and rotting floorboards.

"Be careful," I said, picking my way across them to the

staircase. When I reached the first step, I put my foot out, testing whether or not it would take my weight. It seemed quite sturdy, perhaps the only thing in the house that did, and I started to ascend. Serena and Vita followed closely behind. When I reached the last step, there was nothing except the top of the ceiling, with a perfectly square board cut into the plaster. With some trepidation, mainly nervousness about the possibility of humongous rats, I pushed against it. It gave way easily, setting a smattering of dust and plaster debris on top of our heads. I coughed, my eyes stinging as the grime covered me.

"I'm going to need another shower," I said, looking down at my filthy hands and feet. I hoped they had shoes up here too. If we were going to get out of here eventually, I'd rather not traipse about the jungle in bare feet.

With a final push, I moved the board to the side and clambered up into the attic.

"What did I tell you!" Serena announced as she climbed up behind me. The attic was surprisingly full of light. The ceiling had skylights built into it, bathing the room in sunshine, but also making it the temperature of a furnace.

"Let's open them," I replied, already starting to feel beads of perspiration rolling down my back. We each took one of the four windows, pushing against them with effort. One wouldn't budge at all, no matter how hard we tried, but the other three did—letting in slightly cooler air than below in the gardens.

I looked around the attic. It was full of heavy-looking chests, more paintings covered with mildewed sheets, broken chairs, side tables and lamps. There was even a haggard-looking rocking-horse in the far corner, one of its eyes popped out, with stuffing falling from the socket. I shuddered.

Why is this place so consistently creepy?

Serena moved over to one of the chests, flicking the latch up and pushing it open. More groans emanated from the hinges, but then the lid swung open with a heavy thump.

"Bingo," she called out, already rifling through its contents.

"Oh, you have *got* to be kidding me," I remarked as she pulled out a large, yellow-white petticoat.

"Come on, what did you expect?" she replied with a grin.

"Does anyone else really miss Corrine?" Vita added as she tentatively held up the hem of the petticoat by the tips of her fingers. Serena dropped it back, pulling out more items—bodices, more whitish undergarments, silk dresses, cotton pinafores, and men's items too, shirts and trousers. They looked the most normal of the lot, but there probably wouldn't be enough menswear to go around, as the boys would need most of it.

After a few minutes, we'd managed to make three piles— one of the menswear items that we'd take down to the others, one of clothing that under no circumstances would any of us be caught dead in, and a pile, mostly of undergarments, that we thought were viable options—they looked like they'd cover enough of the body to be acceptable, but were less thick than the outer layers.

"I can't understand how they wore so many clothes back then," I murmured in astonishment. "Underwear that's basically a full outfit, and then more layers on top of that."

Vita shrugged, eyeing the outfits warily. "I guess they were just used to it. But you're right. I couldn't imagine ever wearing so much stuff…getting ready must have been exhausting."

"Servants," Serena replied. "They probably helped. And I guess in those days, the women just sat around looking pretty."

I held up one of the more flouncy, silk ensembles.

"I do declare, Draven, you are *mighty* fine," I crowed in

my best Southern drawl.

Serena was not impressed. She rolled her eyes at me and snatched the dress out of my hands, dumping it back into the 'don't even go there' pile.

"Shut it," she replied.

I batted my eyelids, laughing.

"You've got to admit—both he and Bijarki are handsome specimens. And unless I'm mistaken, the Druid seems particularly fond of *you*."

"Only because I've spent the most time with him," Serena retorted, her cheeks aflame. "It's not a big deal. Plus, he saved my life—so I can't help but feel a bit of appreciation for him, can I?"

"It's not a criticism," I replied with a grin. "I'm warming to the Druid anyway. I think he's genuinely trying to help us."

"Me too," Vita added. She swiftly changed the subject, picking up a few of the undergarments. "Let's try some of these on, see if they fit."

Serena nodded gratefully, pulling out the nearest dress. A few moments later we were all looking at one another and grinning at our appearances. We looked a bit like Amish women—the dresses were a simple white cotton, tight at the bodice, but respectfully so, and then flowing down into loose skirts. They weren't ideal, but they would be better than wearing our pajamas constantly, and would probably be a bit cooler.

"Actually, I have to say, both of you look really good," Serena observed, her grin growing wider as Vita twirled around in the dress.

"Same to you," I replied truthfully. The dress matched her alabaster skin, and made her shock of black hair stand out all the more. She was so small that the bodice was slightly loose on her, but other than that, the dress fit perfectly.

"Let's get downstairs," Serena stated. "The others will be waiting, we can try the rest on later."

I scooped up the men's stuff, while Serena and Vita carted the rest of the acceptable garments off between them. I took one look around the attic before heading back down the staircase. It was roomy and spacious, and I liked the vast amounts of light it got compared to the rest of the house. If we were going to be staying here any longer, I wondered if it would be a more suitable place for us to sleep.

"What's up?" Serena asked, noticing my hesitation.

"Just thinking it's the nicest room in the house…if we

were staying any longer, I'd suggest moving up here."

"I was thinking the same," she agreed. "I guess it just depends what's going to happen next."

I nodded, glancing at both the girls.

How much longer *would* our stay be?

Vita

Once we'd dropped off the clothes with the others and had breakfast, it was time for another training session with the Druid. This time, instead of taking us down into the basement, he led us outside. Bijarki followed behind him, both carrying bags of equipment that Draven had told us were for the session.

As soon as I'd seen Bijarki at the breakfast table, I regretted my choice of attire. It seemed to please him, his eyes travelling from my bare feet, as we hadn't managed to find any shoes yet, up to the slightly revealing bodice. He abruptly looked away as Draven cleared his throat. I had flushed, feeling strangely light-headed, and eaten my breakfast in silence.

As soon as we were outside, I felt better. The air seemed a bit fresher today, and I was glad that we would be outside in the sunshine rather than cooped up in the airless and damp basement.

I watched Draven and Bijarki as they emptied the contents of the bags on the grass. There were six copper balls, each with small holes in the top of them, with a solid base. Next, they pulled out clumps of dried herbs—the herbs smelled earthy and sweet, but I didn't recognize them at all. Draven opened up the balls, unscrewing the top from the bottom. Inside each he stuffed handfuls of the herbs and then lit a match, enflaming them before screwing the two parts back together.

"What are those?" I asked curiously.

"They are censers. Used to burn herbs and incense so that it flows directly upward," he replied, screwing the top onto the last ball. I peered over them, instantly hit with an almost intoxicating wave of smoke and the herbs' heady fragrance.

"Stand back for now," the Druid warned me. "I need to explain first."

He called the others over, and we gathered around the

copper spheres.

"You already know what it's like to slip into the semi-conscious state," Draven began, addressing Aida, Phoenix and me. "Now that you know what it feels like, we're going to try a different, less invasive method, which will guide you into that state, rather than force you to be in it. So you will need to do the work."

"And we couldn't do this before because..." Aida asked sarcastically.

"Because you weren't ready," Draven snapped back. "The fumes of the herbs will help you. All that's required is that you inhale them, and try to ease your mind into a meditative state."

"Hang on a second," Serena asked, interrupting, "these herbs—they're not hallucinogens or anything like that, right?"

The Druid frowned. "No, of course not. The herbs actually produce their own energy. They're called *Taqa*, and the plant they're derived from is very rare and much sought-after. The energy will help focus your abilities, almost as if you are inhaling a botanical life force."

I raised my eyebrows in surprise. If the herbs were that potent, no wonder they were heavily sought after. It was starting to look like I could learn a lot from Draven, and the idea pleased me. It would be good to learn while I was here—take some of the mysteries of the In-Between home with me, when the time came.

If it ever comes.

I shoved the bleak thought aside, and refocused on Draven and the herbs.

"Sit on the ground," he informed us, "and inhale. Your bodies will do the rest."

I did as I was asked, slowly moving into a cross-legged position and breathing in as much as I could of the steady wisp of smoke that emanated from the spheres. Instantly I started to feel drowsy, my mind foggy as if I was in a deep sleep—but, strangely, remaining fully conscious. I supposed the closest thing I could compare it to was having a particularly lucid dream.

I watched as Phoenix's eyelids closed, and he dropped backward into the grass. It alarmed me slightly, but didn't break the hold the herbs had over me, and soon I felt my own eyelids growing heavy. I submitted to the effects, and felt my body fall backwards in the same manner. It was strange. Where the ground was meant to hit my back, there was an absence of solidity, so I felt like I was falling backward through the earth, tumbling down, down, further into a dark void of nothing.

I landed on something hard, the back of my skull slamming against it, making my head ring. I immediately sat up and looked around. I was in exactly the same place as I was in my previous vision, the sky around me star-studded and endless, with its glowing cosmos. I looked behind me, seeing the Oracle in her sphere of water—her eyes wide with warning as they had been before. I quickly turned, looking ahead, just in time to see my friends running down the pathway, heading straight for the Oracle.

I stood up instinctively, waving my arms around for them to stop, before reminding myself that they couldn't see me, and no matter how loud I screamed and yelled, it wouldn't stop what would come next.

Sure enough, the Destroyers appeared over the edge of the cliff. Their horses' wings beat furiously in the night's sky, their black eyes fixed on the rescue party. The spear was thrown. I watched in slow motion as it soared straight through the air—smashing into Jovi and running through him till his body arched backward, impaled on its wooden shaft.

I turned my head away, cursing the vision for showing me this again. I didn't want to see it—I'd *never* wanted to see it.

Screams erupted, and I looked up to see Serena and Aida both launching themselves toward Jovi. I felt like I was underwater, every sound muffled, every movement heavy and labored. I saw, with complete clarity, the pain, shock and surprise on my friends' faces.

Then it all fell silent.

The vision froze. Another spear had been thrown, stopping in mid-air before reaching its target. The Destroyers glared at us all with cruel malice. I heard the shuffle of my own feet on the dew-soaked grass as I moved forward, reaching out to touch Jovi.

His face was barely recognizable in that moment, his mouth open as he cried out, his eyes wide and fearful. Not fear of the spear, or the Destroyers at the cliff edge, but as if he was recognizing his own death, staring it in the face as his body let him down, as if he'd never before realized that he was mortal.

Is this what death looks like?

Was it that frightening to face your own end? Like Jovi, like us all, I had never really considered my own death—

not when we lived in the safest place on Earth. And most of us in The Shade were immortal anyway, or had such long lives it felt that way.

A voice, coming from the water-filled sphere, interrupted my morbid musings.

"Vita?"

I spun around, facing the Oracle. While everything else was still frozen, she alone seemed to be moving in her glass prison. Her hair wafted out gently behind her, and when she opened her mouth, bubbles rose to the surface.

"Vita, is that you?"

I nodded, my heart pounding in my chest as I took a step closer toward her. I froze completely as her body started to move...or not. It was confusing. The Oracle remained where she was, but a white, faded replica of her being stepped out from the glass constraints of the sphere. She looked like a ghost, and through her non-corporeal form I could see the 'real' Oracle still floating behind her. The ghost of the Oracle walked toward me, her eyes still unseeing, the runes moving rapidly over her body. Her hair was wet, leaving drips of water on the grass.

"Vita, answer me," she pleaded, her voice barely above a whisper.

"I'm here," I answered, my voice high-pitched and wavering.

She closed the space between us and stood inches in front of me. Her hands latched onto my arms. Her fingers were ice cold, so cold I felt like they almost burned marks onto my skin.

"Vita, listen to me. Time is running out. You need to find the Daughters, they will help, but you need to act fast. The Druid isn't as safe as he thinks."

She abruptly dropped my arms, looking up at the sky. I followed her gaze, but could see nothing. When I turned back to face her, the apparition was gone, and only the Oracle in the sphere remained.

"Wait!" I called out, running across the grass to reach the temple. I didn't get very far before I started to feel nauseous, my head spinning. The vision was coming to an end.

SERENA

Even out in the bright sunshine that seemed to give the illusion of safety—or at least it was more comforting than the surroundings of the basement—watching my brother, Vita and Aida slowly pass into an unconscious state was an uncomfortable moment. Draven told us to avoid the fumes ourselves, but even so I could feel myself growing slightly drowsy as the herbs' aroma wafted my way with the breeze.

"How are they doing?" Bijarki asked, watching Vita.

"They're fine," Draven replied, his eyebrows raised in a warning as he saw where his friend's attention was directed.

"They seem to be pretty out of it," murmured Jovi. His

gaze was directed at Draven, his brow furrowed in an expression of distrust.

"I'm sure it's fine," I said, soothing Jovi. He nodded with some reluctance and then took a step back to watch with Field, who hadn't moved an inch or said a word from the moment our friends had gone under.

I could see all of their chests rising with steady, sleep-like breaths, and the repetition and calm of the motion started to relax me.

"Draven!" Bijarki barked as he moved swiftly over to my brother. I had been watching Vita, but I turned instantly to Phoenix, seeing his body twitching.

"What's happening?" I asked, placing my hands on either side of his arms. His skin was ice cold beneath his shirt, but he was also sweating profusely.

Draven placed a palm across his forehead, muttering something under his breath.

"What?" I asked, panicked. It was no time for the Druid to be evasive. If there was something wrong with my brother, I wanted to know, *now*.

"Dammit!" the Druid swore, throwing the censers with the smoking herbs away from Phoenix's body.

"Tell me what's happening!" I tried to shake my brother,

hoping that he would wake, but the Druid yelled at me to stop. Jovi grabbed me by both shoulders, moving me back and away from Phoenix.

"Get off," I cried, twisting out of his grasp.

"It's because he's a syphon—I forgot." The Druid let out another volley of curses.

"Syphon? You mean a sentry!"

"And your primary ability is to *syphon*," he growled back at me. "He has taken in too much of the herb. I should have predicted this! It's an energy herb—his body thinks it's food."

I realized what the Druid was saying. Phoenix had not only inhaled the herb like the others, his instincts must have kicked in as well, and so his body had started to syphon up the fumes, eager for the energy they would provide.

"So what's happening?" I cried. "What do we do now?"

"It needs to get out of his system. Bijarki, Field, Jovi—move his body closer to the house and out of the direction of the breeze. He needs clean air."

I staggered back up to my feet, following them as they heaved Phoenix's frame over toward the greenhouse.

Phoenix's body continued to twitch, moving more violently with every passing second.

"What can I do?" I turned to Draven, my eyes pleading. "Please, tell me what I can do!"

"The herbs are now at a level where they're poisonous," he replied, not looking me in the eye. "It's going to be causing him great pain—which will make things much worse. His body is cramping up, when it needs to relax in order to expel the poison. Have you ever tried to syphon pain away?" he asked.

"What? No! It doesn't work like that," I retorted angrily.

"It can, I assure you. I have met other creatures with syphoning abilities, and it should work the same way. I just don't think you've tried before."

"Then show me how," I replied swiftly, willing to try anything, no matter how ludicrous the idea seemed.

The Druid took my hands in his strangely rough ones. Together we knelt down on the floor, his eyes now fixed on mine, not flinching as he met my panicked gaze.

"You need to stay calm. Breathe for a moment."

I did as he asked, my breath only hitching once, when my brother cried out—an undistinguishable guttural sound, indicating that his pain was worsening.

"I'm ready," I replied firmly.

"Place your hands across his chest. Try to find the pain

in his mind, and remove it—taking on part of it."

I nodded, doing what he'd told me. Phoenix's chest was as ice-cold as the rest of him, and my arms trembled as I touched him, so frightened that he wouldn't make it. That I wouldn't be able to help.

I closed my eyes, focusing solely on my brother and letting my surroundings blur and melt away. I could feel his mind—jagged, pained, my vision filled with red and black as my energy reached out toward his. But Draven was right. I could feel his pain. It was like a black poison in his mind, vicious and bitter. I started to syphon it off him, focusing only on the poison, so I wouldn't sap his energy. Eventually I could feel it becoming my own—my head throbbing with his pain, my veins filling up with its acid poison.

Phoenix stopped twitching. I opened my eyes, watching as his face relaxed from its contortion, soon looking like he was back in a state of dream-filled sleep. I took the last of what my body could hold of his pain, and a moment later, while I was still reeling from its effect, his eyelids fluttered open.

It worked.

SERENA

I felt sick. The sensation had been such an unpleasant one, and I couldn't seem to get rid of the feelings that were circulating my body, leaving every limb feeling heavy and dead.

"*What* was that?" Phoenix asked groggily as he moved to sit up.

"Wait a bit," Field replied, easing my brother back down onto the ground.

"I'm sorry," Draven replied evenly. "I didn't realize it would have that effect on you—you took too much of the herb in. It toxified your bloodstream. It will be out soon, there won't be any permanent damage."

"And you're sure of that this time?" I couldn't help but snap. The Druid had pushed me too far—endangering my brother's life like that was unacceptable. He should have told us that the herb could be poisonous in large quantities so at least we could have been forewarned that it was dangerous.

"I am sorry," Draven replied. "I should have thought more carefully."

"Yeah, you should have," I agreed.

"The others are fine," Bijarki added, gesturing to Aida and Vita still sleeping peacefully in the grass. "It was an honest mistake."

I shook my head, in no mood to hear the incubus defending his friend.

"Your methods are too dangerous." Jovi joined in, glaring at both the Druid and Bijarki. "We all want answers, but you're rushing them. They're obviously not prepared for this yet! Vita had the first vision on her own, without your so-called 'help'—why not just give them some time to work it out?"

The Druid shook his head.

"We don't have time, Jovi," he bit out. "We're all in

danger. I'm not just protecting my own interests, I'm protecting theirs as well! How many times do I have to tell you that?"

Jovi stayed silent, still glaring at Draven. He shook his head, leaving the rest of us as he made his way over to his sister and Vita.

"Let me help you up," I said, turning to Phoenix. I couldn't even look at Draven. My brother rose to his feet, and silently we walked toward Jovi, Field joining us, and leaving Draven and Bijarki behind.

"They're waking!" Jovi called out, beckoning us over.

I hurried to his side, just in time to see Aida's bright golden eyes open, staring up at the sky. A few seconds later, Vita joined her, sitting bolt upright, her chest heaving as if she'd been running.

"Are you okay?" I asked, crouching down next to her.

We were joined by Draven and Bijarki, both looking expectantly at my friends. I frowned at them both, wishing they'd give us some space.

"I saw the Oracle again," Vita burst out, "it was the same vision as before." She turned to the Druid, her face solemn. "We need to get to the Daughters. The Oracle says you're not safe. We need to find them, they'll help us."

"Are you sure?" Draven asked, his expression perplexed—and worried.

"I'm sure. The Oracle spoke to me directly. I think it's what she wanted to say that time in the bathroom…" Vita trailed off, realizing her mistake. We had kept that information from Draven, not sure whether or not we could trust him.

The Druid's face darkened.

"What time in the bathroom?" he asked, looking around at us all. I sighed, irritated at myself for not telling him earlier. It was something that, on reflection, we probably shouldn't have withheld. I told him briefly what had happened to Vita, and his face darkened further.

"Do you know how much magic she would have used to get in contact with you?" he growled. "More than you could possibly imagine. I would have known from that alone that whatever she was trying to tell you was a life-and-death matter. You *fools*."

"Well, now we know," I replied heatedly. "We didn't know what she was trying to say before—there can't be much harm done."

"I agree with Vita," Aida said, breaking the tension slightly. "We're not safe. In my vision, I saw the Destroyers preparing to hunt. They were given orders from Azazel—he knows we're in Eritopia, and he won't stop searching till he finds us. I know you say this house is safe, but…I don't know. It's just a feeling I have that something's going to go horribly wrong."

Aida's words chilled me to the bone.

"What about you, Phoenix?" I asked quietly. "Did you even have a vision?"

"What happened?" Aida asked, before my brother could reply. I glared at Draven, waiting to fill her in, but he just stared back at me with equal ferocity. I told the others what had happened, and was only slightly rewarded when both Vita and Aida shot Draven looks of disgust.

"It was an accident," Phoenix replied, placing a hand on my arm. "He didn't mean it. And yes, I did have a vision, another dud though. This time I was underground, standing in a chamber of soil—I could even see earthworms moving about in it. It was pretty repulsive, actually. But in the middle of the chamber, there was a huge shell. Like a regular snail's shell, except it looked like it was made of pearl, all pink and white. It glowed, I think." Phoenix shook his head, "it was weird. But nothing else happened… That was all I saw."

"I wonder why you saw her," Draven breathed.

"Huh? Her? What do you mean?" my brother replied, looking bemused.

"You saw the last Daughter of Eritopia. The Daughter I am sworn to protect, in payment for the security of this house." Draven replied slowly. His gray eyes seemed to dull, as if he was a million miles away, remembering another time.

"I don't understand," I replied, feeling utterly bewildered. So many questions crowded my mind that I was momentarily paralyzed as to which to ask first. "Phoenix said he saw a *shell*. What are you talking about— '*last Daughter*?'"

"As I said," Draven said, almost growling in impatience as he returned to the present, his eyes piercing mine. "There is much, *much* that you are still to learn about the In-Between and the species that inhabit it—especially the Eritopian galaxy." He paused, drawing in a breath through his nose. "The Daughters are... almost like the harpy species you might have come across in your dimension, in that they are not birthed normally, but rather hatched. That *shell* Phoenix saw is in fact an egg."

I exchanged a glance with Field at the mention of the

word harpy, who was still looking just as confused as I felt. "So that egg is hidden somewhere in this house, and you're protecting it?" I asked. "And the Daughters—they're like some kind of bird creatures?"

"It is not of relevance to you where the egg is," he replied, frowning. "And they do not resemble birds, but I can assure you they have the temperament of a harpy."

I felt snubbed at his dismissal of my first question, but continued questioning, "Why do you say 'last' Daughter? Why wouldn't there be more?"

"Again like harpies, their birth is unconventional—and something of a mystery. The legend goes that all the Daughters in existence today were from a single batch of eggs left on a mountain in a distant Eritopian star, many many dawns ago… Nobody I've ever come across knows what kind of creature laid the eggs, and apparently, neither do the Daughters themselves. There was a single egg that remained unhatched, however, and that is what the Daughters wish to protect in these turbulent times—they consider it… highly valuable, and the Daughters would not want Azazel getting a hold of it, in case he wished to use it for some kind of power play."

I stared, dumbstruck, beginning to understand why

Draven was slowly drip-feeding us information about Eritopia and the In-Between … this place and its inhabitants truly were another world away from what GASP was used to dealing with. We were in utterly unchartered waters.

"Why would the Daughters ask you to protect one of their own?" Phoenix asked, composing himself more quickly than the rest of us. "Aren't they all-powerful or something?"

The Druid shook his head.

"Even they feared Azazel—they worried they would be unable to guard her themselves, since they are usually preoccupied with… other matters. They feared that if he knew about her, he would come hunting relentlessly, and nothing would stop him until he had her. They needed one safe, stable place to store the egg."

"But that's putting you in a risky situation," I said, finding my voice again. "Considering you were trying to protect the Oracles, I would have thought that alone would be enough to provide security for this place, regardless of whether or not the egg was here?"

"In truth, the Daughters help no one," Draven replied. "They do not get embroiled in taking sides, and live to guard the region as a whole. In short, they would not have given me this safe haven had they not wished to protect something of their own."

I nodded, slowly grasping the concept, but now worried that we were supposed to go and ask them for help. From the expression on his face, the Druid seemed to be thinking along the same lines as he turned to Vita, asking her more questions about her vision.

"Did anything strike you as strange… *different* from your last vision?" he asked.

"It was clearer, I suppose," Vita replied, wrinkling her nose as she tried to recall it. "And at some point, everything went in slow motion, and the Oracle stepped out from the weird glass that she was encased in—like a ghost. That was different."

Draven nodded, listening to Vita carefully.

"What are you thinking?" I asked.

"I'm not entirely sure yet," he replied. "But I'm hoping this isn't a trick of Azazel's. That he's managed to manipulate your vision. It just seems so strange that the Oracle would ask us to go to the Daughters for help."

"Azazel can manipulate our visions?" Aida burst out, jumping to her feet as if she was readying herself for an imminent attack.

"He has done it before," he replied quietly.

"When?" I demanded.

Draven shook his head, and I huffed in frustration. Another vital question going unanswered.

"It makes no difference right now," he snapped. "You're new to visions. Even a lifelong Oracle wouldn't be able to tell if he had managed to worm his way into her mind. Just leave it for now, Serena."

I stayed silent, angry, but also realizing that the subject had hit a nerve.

"Draven, please," Vita announced. "We need to see the Daughters. I believe the Nevertide Oracle—and if you'd been there, you would too. You're in danger. We all are."

AIDA

After everyone had calmed down, and both Phoenix and Serena had recovered from Phoenix syphoning more of the herbal incense than he should have, we disbanded. Vita and Serena returned inside the house with the Druid and Bijarki, trying to persuade them to visit the Daughters, while the rest of the boys went back upstairs to shower and grab some sleep.

I wasn't ready to return inside yet. I wanted the sun on my face for a bit longer. Maybe if I stayed out here long enough, I could bleach away the memories of my vision like an old photograph.

The Destroyers in my vision had been even more repugnant than the one I'd seen torturing the poor Druid. If that was even possible. I guessed it was seeing them all en masse—the horses neighing with horrid screams, and their long, scaled tails wrapped around them, taking away their breath, as if they might crush their bones and organs at a moment's notice. I had also been taken aback by the size of their army—it had been large, about one hundred of them, standing at attention as Azazel set out his commands to hunt us down.

They'd roared viciously, honoring their leader, whom they were obviously devoted to. Their cries were bloodthirsty and cruel. Their spears had rattled together in the air, each wooden shaft carved into a pointed end, with a purple substance oozing off the tip.

"Are you all right?" Field asked, interrupting me. I almost jumped out of my skin, since I hadn't heard him approach. "You seemed a bit quiet earlier."

"It's just the visions," I replied, trying to sound more upbeat than I felt. "They're not exactly pleasant. I kind of envy Phoenix seeing trees and *eggs*. It would be a lot easier to take."

Field nodded in understanding, his aquamarine eyes

shaded by his hand as he peered down at me. I couldn't help but notice that this was the second time Field had checked up on me after a vision—yesterday and now today. I didn't want to read too much into it, but I couldn't help but feel a bit flattered, and taken by surprise at the attention.

"It worries me that the Oracle doesn't think we're safe here," I said, wanting to continue the conversation—suddenly desperate not to be left alone with my thoughts.

"Me too," Field agreed. "But other than visiting the Daughters, I'm not sure we can do much about it. We'd be in more danger if we left."

"Are you still going to sleep outside?" I asked, wondering if he thought it would be too risky with the Destroyers on the warpath. In truth, I wanted very much to dissuade him from the idea.

"Yeah, probably," he replied with a boyish grin. "I hate sleeping indoors, and this place? Worse than most. I'll stay on the roof."

I nodded, understanding why someone would want to avoid the house, but wishing he wouldn't all the same.

"We're thinking of taking the attic," I replied. "The three of us. It gets more light than the other rooms. I think it will help."

"I know the room you mean, with the skylights in the ceiling?"

"Yeah."

"Nice." He frowned for a brief moment, and then glanced up toward the roof of the house. "Want me to show you the view?"

"What, up there?" I asked.

"Yeah. It's not like we can go anywhere else. Want to see?" he asked again, and I nodded, trying not to look too delighted.

Act casual.

He held out his arms, and I stepped toward him. I stood, awkwardly, so intimately close to him that I could see the skin at his throat and his Adam's apple moving as he told me to hold on tight. His arms closed around me, making my skin tingle, every cell in my body feeling like it was coming alive. My head was pushed against the granite of his chest, and I could feel the steady thump of his heart in its chamber. I inhaled, closing my eyes briefly as his wild scent consumed me.

Very quickly, he jumped up and I felt the weightlessness of us soaring up toward the top of the house. All too soon, my feet hit the rooftop and Field released me, taking a step back and looking around. We had landed on a small square, surrounded by chimney pots. The rest of the roof sloped downwards, but there were a few parts of the house that had either been built later than the original construction, or had been purposefully designed to make the house look grander, which made up a few different rooftops. Some were flat enough to allow us to climb across.

"Nice view, huh?" he said, pointing off into the jungle and the mountain range beyond it. It was beautiful.

"Incredible," I murmured, averting my eyes from Field.

"And this is the attic over here." He beckoned me to follow him as he made his way to the furthest end of the roof. I followed the pinnacle of two slopes, which had enough room for me to walk if I put one foot directly in front of the other.

"Don't worry, I won't let you fall," Field added as he turned to see my much slower progress to our destination.

I nodded, not really hearing him as I focused on my footwork, and soon I was standing by his side, peering down into the attic. We had left the windows open this morning, and I realized that from the position on the roof I could see a lot more of the attic than I could from inside it.

"Look at that," I said, crouching down closer to the widow, reluctantly moving my palm across the dirty glass pane.

"Where?" Field asked, coming beside me.

I pointed to a painting at the back of the room, hidden behind an old chest of drawers. It was an image of a woman, and her face stared out at us, with very pale eyes. She looked solemnly at the artist, reclining on a chair with her hands placed demurely on her lap.

"Do you think it's the other Oracle, Elissa?" I asked.

"I'm guessing so," Field replied.

She also had no breasts to speak of, though the shadows of runes that were typically associated with the Oracles were gone. Perhaps this was the artist, or even the subject's desire, though. It didn't mean she hadn't had them.

"I'll ask Phoenix later if he recognizes her," I decided. "But I wonder why it's not hanging up somewhere? Phoenix said that Draven and Elissa were close...why would he hide this away?"

Field shrugged, moving away from the window.

"We still don't know exactly what happened to her. It might have been painful for him to keep it up after she was gone."

Perhaps Field was right. I hadn't actually asked Serena what she'd found in the diary since we last spoke to her. I hoped she was a little closer to uncovering the mystery of Elissa. I was relying on her to help us in some way—to learn how to regain our sight if we ever lost it.

It was something I didn't really want to think about, and I too turned away from the window, looking out across the jungle.

"It will be all right," Field murmured. I quickly glanced toward him, noticing that he was watching me. His expression was anxious, as I was sure mine was. I appreciated his reassurance, but I wasn't sure that what he said was true. I wasn't sure that things were going to be all right.

Vita

I followed Draven and Bijarki back indoors, with Serena hot on my heels.

"Can you at least explain why we can't see the Daughters?" Serena asked impatiently as we walked through the house. "Or at least tell us what you're so afraid of? Even if they can't help us, there's no harm in asking, right?" She was insistent, and I knew from experience that my friend wasn't going to let the matter drop.

"There's always a price to be paid, Serena," the Druid snapped as we entered the stifling heat of his living room. He paced back and forth, while Bijarki stared into the fire, his expression hard to read. I thought he was angry, not frightened like Serena had suggested, but I didn't understand why.

"If the Oracle says we're not safe, we're not safe," Serena pressed again. I could see she was growing more agitated by the second. It didn't help that the Druid kept pacing, obviously mulling the matter over, but he kept us all shut out.

I moved to stand by the door to the basement. The cold air from below whistled through the door, so it was the only place I could be in the room without fainting. Serena came and stood next to me, moving her cheek to the crack in the doorway while trying to fan herself.

"And will you put the damn fire out already?" she said suddenly, losing her temper.

The Druid stopped his pacing and looked at her in amusement. I didn't know what he thought was so funny, but Serena's outburst seemed to have done the job.

"All right," he replied with some reluctance. "I agree with you, we're not safe here. We should probably speak to the Daughters."

"You don't know what you're asking," Bijarki snapped, glaring at Serena. "None of you do."

"Silence," Draven retorted, glaring at his friend.

Bijarki shook his head in disgust, and turned his attention back to the fire. I didn't understand his outburst—and so far, no matter how fraught the tension in the house had been, the incubus had kept his cool...why was this bothering him so much? Whatever it was, the consequences of paying a visit to the Daughters must be severe, and the thought made me uneasy. The comparison Draven had drawn between them and harpies wasn't exactly comforting...

"We just need to make sure we're asking the right question," the Druid asserted more to Bijarki than us, as if he was trying to placate his friend.

"Then we should ask for more protection for the house?" Serena suggested, seemingly oblivious to the tension building between the friends—either that, or she didn't care. "Or, even better, a way to get back to The Shade? I know that GASP would take you both in and offer protection if you wanted."

"How many times do I need to tell you that The Shade isn't safe?" the Druid growled. "They *will* find you there, I promise you that."

"Well, I'm sorry," Serena retorted, "but when you first

told us about the protection of the house, you made it sound like the moment we stepped outside the borders of safety, the Destroyers would find us instantly. Well, we've all left the house, and they didn't hunt us down straight away. Perhaps we can bide our time, build up a stronger protection around The Shade."

"They weren't specifically hunting for you then," the Druid countered, "they are now."

"Then what?" she asked. "What are we supposed to say when we see the Daughters?"

"I don't know," sighed Draven, rubbing his temples in frustration. "But more protection is too vague. We need something concrete, and perhaps a bargaining chip. Something to tempt them."

"Like what?" I asked.

"That I still don't know."

We watched the Druid as he began to pace again, and I raised my eyebrows toward the doorway, hoping Serena would take the hint. We needed to leave the Druid to mull it over. Serena either didn't see me or ignored me, because she interrupted him once again.

"Why don't we just tell them the truth?" she suggested. "Tell them that the Oracle spoke to one of us, and told us to come to them? Surely an Oracle using that much power to contact us is enough of a point of interest for them?"

The Druid stopped his pacing, and looked over at Bijarki. The incubus shook his head at the Druid, and then returned to the fire.

"Let me think about it," Draven replied. "It might work…but I need some time."

"Come on, Serena," I murmured, pulling at her sleeve. We needed to leave the Druid in peace. He obviously wasn't going to tell us anything further, and we were just wasting our time continuing to argue with him.

"Okay," she sighed reluctantly, but followed me out of the room.

"Wait," called the Druid, just as we stepped out onto the hallway. "Vita, I need you to keep trying to get in touch with your visions as best that you can. The Oracle has only appeared to you so far, and I'm beginning to think it's because of your fae blood—you are partly a creature of the In-Between. Try to call her out again, if you're able."

Partly a creature of the In-Between. I had never really thought of myself in those terms before.

I nodded, though I was doubtful I was going to be able to 'call her out,' as he'd put it. My fae traits weren't exactly pronounced—I had thought it was just a coincidence that it had been me the Oracle had called, not because of any latent fae blood. I had actually thought it was odd that she'd contacted me first and not Aida, who so far seemed to be seeing the 'present,' rather than the past or future like Phoenix and me.

"Okay," I mumbled, "I'll try my best."

Serena and I left the room.

I took a lungful of air as soon as we stepped out into the hallway. I'd been so hot my head had started to spin, and I had to pause on the banisters until the black dots dancing in my vision slowly started to fade.

"What is with the heat obsession?" I groaned.

"No idea," Serena replied. "It's crazy. Maybe he doesn't have good circulation or something? I guess he *is* centuries old, even if he doesn't look it," she added doubtfully.

I stared at her in amazement.

"That's not it!" I replied, stifling a laugh. The Druid was one of the most virile males I'd ever seen, easily on the same level of physical fitness as any of the other members of GASP. Derek was even older than he was, and still showed no signs of slowing down. Though, of course, he was a vampire, and immortal. We didn't know enough about the

Druids yet to guess whether they too were immortal, or had extraordinarily long lives like the jinn.

"Have you asked Draven about the Druids yet?" I asked, curious. "Like, what they actually are in detail – their traits and abilities?" Perhaps he and Serena had talked about it already.

"No," she replied with a frown. "He's so evasive…and there's been so much going on. I hadn't even thought to ask. But he's obviously aged, right? Phoenix saw him as a little kid."

I nodded, agreeing.

"He must have been so lonely here," I mused as we walked up the staircase. The house was so oppressive, so silent, even when it was full of people—like the junk and rotting walls sapped the noise and life out of everything.

"I know," she replied quietly. "It's why I think he comes across as so stern and distant. I think he's not used to people, and doesn't exactly know what to do with us."

"I get that impression too. I mean, Bijarki must have spent time here before, but it's not like the two of them exactly have an easy-going relationship. It's more like commander and soldier."

As I said the words, I thought about Bijarki's behavior

just now. It had felt like he was trying to protect the Druid from something concerning the Daughters. It had been unwelcomed, obviously, but the intention was there. I wondered if there was a deeper friendship there, between Draven and the incubus. One that both men navigated awkwardly, having spent both their lifetimes embroiled in a state of danger and war.

"Are you going to try to call on the Oracle?" Serena asked as we reached the top of the hallway. I could see her edging toward Elissa's old room, clearly desperate to continue reading the diary.

"I'll try. Don't worry, I'll call if I need anything, go ahead." Getting back into the right state to receive visions would probably take a while anyway, and I didn't want her impatience stressing me out.

"I'd probably only be annoying," she replied, pulling a face.

"I *know*," I said, pushing her toward the room and laughing.

I headed off to the bedroom, ready to attempt accessing another vision. Already exhausted from the last one, I had serious doubts that I'd manage again today, but I felt that the others were relying on me—too heavily, in fact.

Not for the first time, I wished Zerus was here. I could have done with his guidance, his understanding. I felt strangely lonely, even though I was surrounded by my friends—and it wasn't like I was the only one having visions. I had no excuse or justification for the feeling, just that I felt it. It was painful, and I thought of Draven again, all alone here in this house. I felt a pang of guilt. We had been giving him a hard time, all of us, when he'd only been trying to help.

SEREПA

I took the diary back downstairs, thinking that I'd find a shady spot in the garden to read in. The garden was empty when I arrived, and I wondered where everyone had gone. Assuming they were either in the house somewhere, or around the entrance of the building, I found a magnolia tree to lean up against and opened up the diary again.

Almus has still not returned. It's been three days and I don't know what to do. I haven't had any visions since he left, and so this afternoon I went in search of the herbs that we'd used to invoke my visions when I'd first arrived in Eritopia and fallen ill, halting their regularity for a short period.

I took Draven down to the basement with me, not wanting him to be left alone, but at the same time worried that he'd panic when I fell into a semi-conscious state. Still, I felt the risk was worth it—if anything happened to his father that I could have prevented, I would never forgive myself.

To my regret, none of the visions showed me Almus. I saw plenty of the Destroyers, and Azazel. None of it gave me any hope. I couldn't see an end to their destruction of these planets, and that fleeting glimpse I'd seen of us trekking through the jungle in safety didn't reappear.

Draven was a good boy, and sat silently playing with beakers and herbs while the visions consumed me. I worry about him. What if his father never comes home? Will it just be the two of us, alone in this house? Waiting for the end of days?

I can't believe that's our future.

God, this was depressing. I wanted to skip ahead, find out if Almus returned home to her and his son. I presumed that at some point he had, as he was here later to try to save the second, Nevertide Oracle, but what had happened to Elissa?

I turned the page, seeing another jump ahead in dates— about two months.

I am frightened that Almus will never return.

I am frightened every day. His son will grow up without a father, and I will have to go on without my rock, the man who showed me I could be happy again. The one person I felt saw my soul, who loved me despite the fact I couldn't bear him children, who restored color to my life—literally, when he assisted in restoring my vision. How would I survive without him?

I try to take solace in Draven. I love the child, and I vow to care for him for the rest of my life, whether or not Almus returns to us.

How *exactly* had her vision been restored? I got the impression that fleeting comment was going to be the only answer I got, and it had obviously happened before she started writing the diary, and so was ancient history to her now. *Damn.*

I also felt a huge amount of pity for her. Two months would have been a long time to wait for him. No wonder it sounded like she'd given up hope of him ever returning. I hurriedly read on, desperate for Almus's return. The breeze, thankfully, had started to pick up, sending petals scatting across the pages. I looked up in surprise, amazed to find that the breeze seemed restricted to where I was sitting. The rest of the grass and trees across the garden were perfectly still.

The pages of the notebook ruffled, the pages whipping themselves up into a frenzy. I held on tight to the notebook, waiting for it to pass. Most likely the wind abnormality was just a small, irregular pocket of air bursting out in revolt against the heavy afternoon sun. I tried to refocus on the book, ignoring the strange sense of unease that crept over me.

I have seen him! In a vision, and not a happy one, but at least I know he is alive! I feel like I have gone almost half mad. I am writing this in the middle of the night, having just woken, and I don't know what to do with myself.

Almus was in the jungle somewhere, calling out to me with silent cries, his arms raised—in welcome or warning? I couldn't tell…it was the least vivid vision I have ever encountered. The images confused me, flickers of Almus more than a solid sense of his being. But still it is hope.

I need to decide what I am to do.

Almus always told me never to leave the confines of the house…but what if he needs me? I need to decide before dawn. I am sure I cannot stay here and do nothing—I am prepared to take the risk. But what of Draven? I can't leave him here, but can I take him with me? It seems too dangerous.

He needs to be protected. At all costs. Almus would never

forgive me if anything happened to him. What do I do? Oh, diary, I wish you could tell me.

I heard noises coming from the greenhouse, and with reluctance I drew my eyes across the garden to see who it was. It was Jovi and Field. They waved to me, and started to make their way over.

"The diary?" asked Jovi as they approached.

"Yeah. It's just getting good."

"We won't disturb you then. We were going to have a training session," he added, slapping Field's back and sending the Hawk stumbling forward.

"You're going to pay for that," Field mocked, dragging him down into a headlock.

"Where's Phoenix?" I asked. I would have thought that my brother would have wanted to join them.

"Don't know," Jovi replied. "We looked for him, but he's not in the house."

I looked worriedly toward the outskirts of the garden.

"He wouldn't," Field replied, understanding my thought process. "I wouldn't worry about him, he's probably gone in search of that tree."

I let out a breath. Field was right. I'd even told him to do that myself.

"We can look for him out front if you want?" Jovi asked.

"Nah," I replied, shaking my head. Phoenix hated missing out on training sessions, but my brother also liked to spend time alone...or sort of alone. It was usually in the company of a girl who didn't live in The Shade—but I guessed in absence of any available outsiders, he'd gone off hunting for a tree. I smirked. I was sure my brother thought the change of priorities was as ludicrous as I did.

"Give us pointers?" Jovi asked. I rolled my eyes, waving the diary.

"I've got other priorities," I replied.

"Aw, come on. You can stop Field from cheating," Jovi said.

I snorted with derision at that. Jovi knew Field was too honorable to cheat—which was probably why it was so fun to tease him about it.

"What?" Field replied with mock indignation.

"I'll watch," I replied, "only to keep an eye on Field." I winked at Jovi and the two of them headed off to a clearing in the grass where they wouldn't be in danger of accidentally hitting me.

I watched them for a while, laughing as they took turns knocking one another to the ground, their punches and throws echoing around the stillness of the garden. I imagined that the force they battered one another with would have been surprising for anyone who wasn't a supernatural, but I was used to the excessive supernatural strength they both displayed.

After a while, I turned toward the greenhouse, sensing another presence. It was Draven, leaning on the broken doorframe, watching the boys as they fought. Field must have noticed him too, because a moment later, he called out to him.

"Want to join us, Draven?" he called, his smirk challenging but not unkind. Jovi frowned briefly, but his sense of competition won him over, and he grinned at the Druid, beckoning him over.

"All right," Draven drawled, making his way over. "Who's first?"

Field and Jovi glanced at one another, Jovi smiling broadly.

"I'm taking you down," Jovi replied, the two of them having reached some kind of agreement. Field backed off and came to sit under the shade of the tree next to me.

"This should be good." He whipped off his sweat-drenched shirt, revealing his muscled torso.

I smiled in agreement. I wasn't worried that the Druid wouldn't be able to handle himself. I'd seen what he was capable of in the forest, though that was with magic…but those muscles, and that broadness. I was pretty sure it wasn't just there for show. Jovi would have a fight on his hands—an entertaining one for Field and me, as Jovi was sometimes too cocky for his own good.

The two men started to circle each other, each weighing up their opponent. I wished Aida and Vita were here to watch this—they'd both get a kick out of it.

The fight started swiftly. Jovi hit first, sending the Druid reeling backward, but at the last moment he caught his footing and caught Jovi's shoulder as the werewolf was about to land another blow. Jovi staggered to the ground, and without a second to recover, Draven sent him flying backward with a kick to the chest. Jovi landed on the earth, laughing. He was quick to jump back up, catching Draven in a mid-air jump and throwing him to the ground. Draven rolled, narrowly avoiding a kick. The Druid scrambled to his feet, launching into another attack. The first blow was blocked by Jovi, but the second landed—sending Jovi to the ground once again. This time the Druid managed to pin him down, and Jovi bellowed a surrender. The Druid instantly backed off, holding out his hand. Jovi took it, launching himself to his feet.

I couldn't help but smile. Both of the men were laughing, and I'd never heard Draven make that sound before, or seen how his face transformed from the stern, focused expression—which usually gave him an air of dignity and coldness—to the handsome, laughing one that I saw now, one that made him look younger, freer somehow. I was struck by how little we knew of Draven—not just what Vita and I had been discussing earlier about the Druids in general, but Draven as a person. As a man—one I wanted to know better.

The fight continued. This time, Field jumped up, swapping places with Jovi. The werewolf came to sit down next to me, grinning.

"He handed you your ass." I laughed.

"I know it," Jovi replied easily. "He's good. I didn't expect that. I know he's built, but he just didn't seem the type."

Jovi wiped a shower of sweat off his brow, flinging it in my direction.

"Eugh! Jovi!" I cried, backing away from him in horror. He laughed, flicking his hands toward me. "Stop!" I laughed, scrambling to my feet. I happened to glance over at the fight as I did so, and for a split second I saw the Druid staring at us with an unfathomable expression before Field, taking his distraction as an opportunity, flung him to the floor. I turned back to face Jovi, who hadn't noticed Draven's look, but had thankfully given up trying to terrorize me with his sweat.

I took my seat back, watching the fight as it resumed like nothing had happened—Draven's focus was solely on Field.

SERENA

When the boys were finished, it was approaching sunset and I decided to go indoors. I was starting to get hungry, and figured the three of us could have an early dinner if the food was ready.

I left before Jovi and Field who were still messing around—Draven had already retreated into the house—and made my way inside. When I reached the main entrance, I heard the creak of floorboards coming from above me, and assumed it was one of the girls. I climbed the staircase, but as I reached the top it was Bijarki I saw instead.

"What are you doing up here?" I asked. He was looking

distinctly shifty, and I knew he'd been caught doing something he shouldn't, whatever it was.

"Just getting a book," he replied smoothly, taking what looked like a random one from the bookshelf next to him.

"On what?" I asked, challenging him. With a roll of his eyes, he looked down at the cover.

"The Kelpie," he replied, holding out the cover of the book for me to see. I read the cover. *The Sea Dwellers, a short history on the Kelpie.* I wondered if those were the In-Between's equivalent to merfolk.

"Really, why?" I asked.

"The conversation yesterday. I thought I could regale you all with interesting facts on Eritopia's creatures."

"*Right*," I muttered, shoving past him on my way to our bedroom—the direction from which he'd emerged. I burst inside and shut the door firmly behind me. Vita and Aida were both fast asleep, sprawled out on the bed. I looked around the room—nothing *seemed* amiss. I didn't trust that incubus in the slightest. I just knew he'd been in here, but I didn't know why.

"Hey," yawned Vita, waking.

"Hey," I replied. "Are you okay?"

She looked around the room, disorientated.

"Oh, damn. I was trying to get in touch with my visions…I must have dropped off," she said sheepishly.

"Don't worry, and don't exhaust yourself—you've done enough today." I was all for them both getting as much rest as they could. The visions were clearly taking a toll on both of them, and I wasn't comfortable with it. I knew we needed them to help us get out of here, but I didn't want them to damage themselves in the process. I could already sense that their energy was low. Normally their vibrancy slammed into me whenever I saw them, but the last two days, their energy had started to diminish. It wasn't a good sign.

Vita still seemed flustered, and a pink glow appeared on both her cheeks.

"Are you sure you're okay?" I asked again, looking at her closely.

"Yeah," she replied quickly. "Just some…weird dreams."

"About the Oracle?"

She shook her head. "No. Erm, they were just weird. About boring stuff—you know, usual weird dream stuff."

"Right," I replied slowly. That girl was so odd sometimes. I didn't imagine for a moment that Vita had ordinary dreams. I couldn't even imagine what it was like up there in that head of hers.

"I'm going to take a shower," she asserted, jumping up off the bed.

"Oh, my God, guys, can you keep it down?" Aida groaned, thumping her pillow.

"Sorry," I replied, as Vita crept off to the bathroom. I came and sat down on the bed, leaning back against the headboard.

"What time is it anyway?" Aida asked, her tone sullen.

"I thought we could have dinner soon," I replied, knowing that the mention of food would probably cheer her up.

"That would have worked if I didn't know that dinner consists of the same food we had last night, and the night before," she replied, reading my mind, but now grinning reluctantly.

"It's still food," I sighed.

"Did you find out anything more about the Daughters?" Aida asked.

I shook my head. "No. But Elissa's diary is getting more interesting—I think I'm close to understanding what happened to her. The subject of sight restoration came up, but apparently, it was Almus, Draven's father, who helped it happen."

"Really?" she replied, sitting up. "That's odd."

"Yeah, I know. I just hope the magic hasn't been lost…that Draven might be able to do the same."

"So do I," Aida replied. "It worries me, a lot. But do you think the Oracle would have passed on the gift in its true form? She must have known that blindness is a sucky deal— no matter if you can see the past, or future or whatever."

"I don't know," I replied. "She might not have known any different. If she was blind from birth, maybe she didn't *know* it was that bad?"

I felt guilty as the words left my mouth—it wasn't exactly an encouraging sentiment—but I didn't want to lie to Aida either. We needed to be prepared for the worst, and hopefully, find a way to stop it.

"And the reproductive organ bit." Aida shuddered. "That would *not* be okay."

I didn't reply. As far as I was aware, from Elissa's diary, she had remained unable to bear children. But surely that was something you had to be born with? Obviously, Aida and Vita both had their reproductive organs—how would that ever change?

"I don't think you need to worry too much about that," I replied, coming to a conclusion. "You have them, you can't just lose them like you can your sight."

"Yeah," replied Aida quietly, "but they can stop working…"

Not knowing what to say, I took her hand and clasped it in mine instead. I wasn't going to let that be my friend's fate. I would move heaven and earth to make sure they didn't have their future children robbed from them.

AIDA

"We're going to see the Daughters tomorrow," the Druid announced as we all sat down to dinner. Serena and Vita turned to him in surprise. I was pleased he'd come to that decision, but considering what the girls had told me about his reluctance earlier, I'd have thought he was going to refuse. I also noticed that Bijarki looked less than pleased. He stared angrily down at his plate, avoiding making eye contact with Draven.

"I'll take you through the process in the morning. You'll need to be ready. It won't be an easy journey, but it's one I think we need to make," Draven continued, his last comment aimed at the incubus. "You'll all need to get a good night's sleep."

"Where are these Daughters?" Jovi asked before I could. "Will we be going through the jungle? The girls will need footwear."

"No," Draven replied. "It's not like that. You'll see tomorrow, but we won't be going through the jungle. There's little chance the Destroyers will be able to sense we've crossed over to their location, otherwise we wouldn't be doing it."

I wondered what he meant by 'crossed over.' Would we be traveling through a portal? I wanted to ask Draven, but I gathered from his expression that he considered the conversation over—we'd just have to wait and see what tomorrow would bring. I was apprehensive, but excited too. I would give anything to get out of the house and have a day of different scenery.

"And these Daughters are dangerous, right?" Field asked.

Before Draven could reply, Bijarki interjected.

"Very. They're deadly creatures," the incubus spat.

Draven looked annoyed at his friend's outburst.

"They're complicated," he replied tersely. "But yes, they can be dangerous. Which is why, tomorrow, I want you to listen very carefully to what I say. You're all going to have to trust me, something you seem to have difficulty doing."

"Not fair," Serena replied calmly. "You took us from the fae star against our will—we weren't exactly inclined to trust you."

Draven nodded, accepting the accusation.

"All right," Field replied, trying to break some of the tension that had started building in the dining room. "We trust you. Now, tell me where you learned to fight like that?"

Jovi and Field both grinned, waiting expectantly for Draven to answer them. I rolled my eyes. Typical that both of them would warm to him after they'd had a training session together. Serena had told me how he'd beat them both pretty soundly.

Draven looked amused at their interest.

"It's science," he replied simply.

"What do you mean?" Jovi asked. "You've got some awesome strength. I felt it, and I'm still feeling it."

"I'm no stronger than either of you," Draven replied. "But I lose less energy by aiming my blows better. If either of you bothered to study anatomy, you'd be the same."

"We have studied anatomy," Jovi replied in confusion.

"Perhaps not the way I have. My study of the body, both humanoid physiques and animal, was all aimed to be used in battle. I can teach you, if you wish?"

"Yes," Field and Jovi replied in unison. I smiled, looking over at Phoenix. Why wasn't he joining in? He'd appeared at dinner, not saying where he'd been, and throughout the meal had sat in near silence, looking like he was a million miles away.

"Phoenix?" I prompted.

"Yeah?" he replied, looking up and around, not aware that it was me who had called his name.

"Are you okay?" I asked.

He looked around—all of us were staring at him. He gave a weak smile. "Sorry— yes to the lessons. If you're as good as these two say you are, I'm all in."

Draven nodded, looking pleased.

"What about you, Bijarki?" Field asked.

The incubus sighed. "I don't think so."

"You think you're too good for us?" Jovi asked jokingly.

"He is," Draven replied with a small smile. "Trust me. The incubi are some of the most fearsome warriors in Eritopia. They can move faster than the undead, be more vicious than the shape-shifters Serena met in the swampland. And that's without their added abilities."

We all turned to Bijarki with a mixture of amazement and trepidation.

"Added abilities?" Vita asked.

It was Bijarki's turn to cast a glance of annoyance.

"Really?" he asked the Druid.

Draven just smirked, leaning back in his chair, evidently enjoying his friend's discomfort. Everyone else was waiting for Bijarki to continue and he looked around at us all with helpless irritation.

"I can affect the thoughts of others," he muttered.

"What do you mean?" Serena asked, her tone sharp.

Bijarki glanced up at her with a wary expression.

"You might understand it as hypnotism, but it is a little subtler than that. It doesn't work on all species—not Druids, for example, much to everyone's disappointment." He glared at Draven before continuing. "But it is effective on a few who prove dangerous to our kind—like the Deargs, Sluaghs, and some others."

Whatever those creatures are…

"Can you hypnotize someone who's sleeping?" Serena asked hotly. I looked over at her, wondering where the question had come from, and why she seemed so flustered.

Vita looked at the incubus with wide eyes, a flush appearing on her cheeks.

Bijarki met Serena's gaze head on, his face also appearing unusually heated.

"Yes," he snapped.

Serena fell silent, but she didn't stop glaring at him for a good few minutes, while the rest of us continued to eat in a confused, awkward silence. Thankfully, it was shortly broken by the Druid rising to his feet and wishing us all a good night.

Once again, he hadn't eaten a thing.

PHOENIX

My sister, Aida and Vita left the dining room first, muttering about Bijarki, Serena shooting the incubus a dark look before she left the room. I didn't understand what had happened there, but I almost felt sorry for Bijarki as he drew himself away from the table and left through another doorway.

Jovi and Field got up to leave next.

"Coming?" Jovi asked. "We should get some rest."

"Yeah," I replied, "you use the showers first. See you up there."

"Okay," he replied, and both of them moved toward the

doorway. I sat looking at the empty table. I didn't feel like sleeping yet. I had found the tree from my vision earlier, out in the front garden. Its boughs had been heavy with blossom, and a stillness and serenity had pervaded it that I'd never encountered before. When I had touched the bark, it had been warm—but that wasn't unusual, the sun was baking…it had just seemed as if the heat was coming from *within* the tree.

I had sat beneath it, as if I was in a trance. I hadn't known how long I'd been there until the sun started to set. I'd somehow managed to spend the entire day there without noticing. The strangest thing was how content I'd felt, as if—out of every single place in the world's dimensions—that was where I was meant to be. It had been even stranger considering that, a few moments before discovering the tree, Eritopia and this crumbling house had been the last place I'd ever wanted to be—I'd had a raging inner dialogue, longing to escape the confines of the house and its overgrown gardens. But when I'd found that tree, I'd felt more at peace with myself and the world around me than I ever had even in The Shade.

There was one thing that had occurred to me while I was sitting at the table.

I stood up, sure that the coast was clear, and made my way to the greenhouse. Draven and Bijarki were nowhere to be seen, and I could hear the sounds of my friends above me, getting ready for bed.

I didn't know why I was so reluctant to tell them I'd found the tree. I knew Serena was desperate to know, but for now, it was something I wanted to keep to myself. Partly because it was all so strange, and I wouldn't really know how to explain how a regular magnolia tree made me feel so much.

Walking swiftly across the gardens, I kept close to the house, hoping Field wouldn't spy me from the rooftops. I strode round the side of the house, eventually reaching the tree. I exhaled in relief. My muscles relaxed—I hadn't realized they had been tensed before this point. I leaned against the bark, closing my eyes briefly before beginning my next task.

It was so obvious, I couldn't understand why it hadn't occurred to me earlier. I looked down at the soil, using True Sight to see the roots of the tree. Slowly they came into vision, twisted and entwined around one another. I followed them down, deeper and deeper into the earth. Their depth wasn't normal—the roots seemed to go on forever. Right at the bottom, I saw what I hoped I would. The roots grasped at a huge shell, the same one I had seen in my vision. It shone brightly, its pearly luminescence making it look like a jewel buried deep in the soil.

Taking a deep breath, and feeling the energy leaving my body as I fought to maintain my sight at such depths, I looked through the casing of the shell, almost blinding myself with the light that emanated from within it. As my eyes adjusted, I started to see the outline of a figure, lying curled up inside the chambers of the shell.

I crouched down lower, and the form started to become clearer. It was a girl, but more than that somehow—she was the most beautiful creature I'd ever beheld, as if she somehow surpassed being generalized by her gender. Her skin was alabaster white, her hair a flaming pinky red that seemed to become part of the shell as she nestled in it, the tips of it reaching down to her feet.

Why is she buried beneath the earth?

I suddenly felt a sharp pang of grief that anyone would cover her with so many layers of earth, that they would hide her from the world when she was so clearly meant to be part of it—to be seen, to let us hear her voice, to watch her walk and move. Her eyes were closed in sleep, and I desperately wanted to know what they would look like, but instead, I had to be content to see her chest rising gently, and the dark lashes on her lids throwing shadows on her cheekbones.

My fingers pressed into the earth. I was ready to dig her up myself then and there, to claw my way through the worm-infested soil that separated us.

"What are you doing?"

I jumped up at the sound of Field's voice. I had been so preoccupied by her beauty that I hadn't heard him approach.

"Just looking at the tree," I replied stiffly. "It's the one from my vision."

"Are you sure?" Field asked, with instant interest.

"I'm sure."

"Can you see anything beneath it? Like the shell you were talking about?"

"No," I replied swiftly.

He looked at me strangely. I realized that my reply had been *too* swift, too dismissive.

"Sorry," I replied, trying to smile. "It's just frustrating. Anyway, I should get some sleep."

"You look tired," agreed Field, looking like he wanted to discuss the tree in more detail, but left it, appearing to ignore my odd behavior and put it down to exhaustion.

"See you in the morning," I said, leaving him standing by the tree. I made my way back around to the greenhouse, hearing the flap of his wings as he ascended to the rooftop. The moment I had left the tree, I felt horribly guilty for lying to him, and not even sure why I'd done it. I wanted to call him back and explain, but something stopped me. I didn't want to share her existence yet, I just wasn't ready. I felt so possessive of her, and protective in a way I couldn't really even begin to explain, not even to myself. I just knew I was supposed to find her. That somehow, we were connected.

I went back inside the house, bewildered and confused. But as I sank into bed, too tired to shower, I realized I felt happier than I could ever remember feeling—like suddenly everything made sense, like I truly belonged somewhere, with someone. With her.

I slept soundly that night, a dreamless sleep that felt closer to death than to life.

SEREПA

I was up early again the next morning, anxious to begin our trip to the Daughters. Like Aida, I was eager to get out of here, even if it was to face creatures that the incubus had deemed 'deadly'.

The incubus in question was starting to become a major problem. Last night, while we'd been having dinner, I'd worked out what he'd been doing up on our floor. As soon as he'd mentioned hypnotism, I recalled what I'd read about incubi in one of Ibrahim's human-written books back in The Shade. It had been an old book on the mythology of supernatural creatures. The author had gotten a great many facts wrong about vampires, werewolves and fae, but I recalled that, as the stories went, incubi usually appeared to their prey in a dream, making humans feel attracted to the creatures before they finally appeared— usually to procreate with them.

A shudder ran through my body. If that was what Bijarki had been doing, then he was in major trouble. I would need to speak to Draven about keeping his friend on a leash. I didn't care if it was his 'natural' inclination—he was to stay as far away from Vita as possible. I'd told both Aida and Vita about my conclusions, but they didn't seem as convinced as I was, though, predictably, Vita had blushed a bright red. Clearly it was up to me to safeguard her against Bijarki. He might have been handsome, and unrelentingly polite and courteous on the surface, but I wasn't convinced. Not by a long shot.

As if I don't have enough things to worry about already.

I waited for the others at the breakfast table, pouring myself a steaming cup of coffee. Field was the first to arrive.

"Did you sleep okay?" he asked, removing the jug of coffee from my place setting with a wry smile.

"I wasn't going to drink it all, but yes, I had a good night's sleep."

He nodded, grinning.

"Before we leave, do you need to syphon off me?" he asked.

I shook my head. I hadn't really had any need to use up my energy here, and when I'd syphoned the pain away from Phoenix, I must have taken a good deal of his energy too. It was my brother I was more concerned about.

"I'm fine, but maybe you could check with Phoenix?" I asked.

"Will do." He nodded. "Did you know he found the tree?"

"No!" I exclaimed. Why hadn't Phoenix mentioned it to any of us?

"Yeah. I saw him crouched in the soil beneath it. To be honest, he was acting oddly. I hope he's all right. He said he didn't see anything beneath it, like the shell—or rather, the egg…but I don't know." Field shook his head, frowning.

"What?" I asked.

"I don't know. Maybe it's nothing… just keep a close eye on him today. He certainly seemed a bit 'off', almost like he was lying to me…But it's Phoenix. He doesn't lie."

I nodded, worried. My brother didn't lie, but then again,

neither did Field. He wouldn't say something like that unless he thought he had good reason to.

"Shall I say something?" I asked.

"Maybe wait till after we see the Daughters. It might be nothing, and I don't want him to think I was spying on him or anything."

"He wouldn't think that," I replied. My brother had a very high opinion of Field and Jovi. He would know that Field was only concerned. Still, perhaps it was best to drop the matter until later. We would have enough to deal with today.

"Are we all ready for the trip?" asked Jovi as he entered the room.

"Ready to get out of here," I muttered.

"The girls and Phoenix not up yet?" Jovi asked me. Before I could reply, Phoenix walked in, looking fresh-faced and clearly in a good mood. I glanced swiftly at Field, who smiled. Clearly whatever had happened last night was in his imagination. I felt it was fine to bring up the subject of the tree, and so I asked my brother about it.

"Yeah, I found it last night," he replied. "I still have no idea what the vision was meant to be showing me, it was just a tree… No shell or egg or anything. Maybe it will all become clearer later."

"Right," I replied, relieved. He seemed perfectly fine, and Field gave a quick nod. We were back to normal.

"Shall I wake Vita and Aida?" I asked, wondering where Draven was. And the incubus…

"Has anyone seen Bijarki?" I asked sharply, rising up out of my seat.

"Here," he replied, appearing behind us and glaring at me. I guessed he picked up on what I'd been thinking—that he was back up in our bedroom, placing dreams inside Vita's subconscious. "Draven requests that you join him in the basement," he added.

"I'll get my sister and Vita up," Jovi said. "Better that my sister's morning mood is inflicted on me."

He left the room, but I stayed seated, wanting to wait for Vita and Aida before we went down.

"We'll be along shortly," I snapped at Bijarki.

"Of course," he replied. "I'll just tell Draven that he needs to wait to begin the perilous mission because some of you can't be bothered to get up." He left the room, banging the door behind him.

"What's his problem?" Phoenix asked, frowning.

"Don't ask," I replied, staring at the closed door.

"Go easy on him, Serena," Field said, his voice gentle but firm. "We can't afford to have friction in this place, we're cooped up in here. If we're at each other's throats, this isn't going to go well."

I bit my lip. I didn't want to tell the boys what I thought he was actually up to. Field had no idea how restrained I was being. I was only keeping quiet because I knew the boys would rip him limb from limb if they knew what he was doing. I wouldn't divulge what I thought until I had some concrete proof.

Soon, Vita and Aida joined us and we all made our way down to the basement. The 'secret' room that led on from the main basement was open, and Draven was already in there with the incubus, deep in conversation. As soon as they heard us approach, they fell silent, and Draven nodded in greeting.

"The process of travel to the Daughters is a fairly complicated one," Draven began, "but if you'll just be patient, I'll explain everything shortly."

I nodded, and we all fell silent, letting the Druid do what he needed to without interruption. I was actually fascinated to see how he *did* travel. Taking us from the fae star must have required a lot of magic and energy to accomplish.

My lips parted slightly as Draven removed his shirt. He had his back to us, and his muscles rippled with the movement over his golden skin. I heard a hiss of breath, but couldn't see what he was doing. Silently, so as to not distract him, I walked around the room, hoping to get a better look. I gasped out loud when I was facing him. In his hand, he had a sharp stone, and was carving symbols across his chest. Blood seeped from each one, but he continued to carve, only the slight flinch of his muscles giving away how painful it must have been. The others followed me, and Bijarki frowned in our direction, warning us to remain silent. Vita and Aida paled, but Jovi looked reluctantly impressed.

When he was finished, Draven let the stone drop to the floor. He held out his hand, and Bijarki quickly handed him a small, stone bowl. Draven held it to his waist, the blood slowly pouring into it.

"W-What are you doing?" I asked, unable to stay silent a moment longer. Draven looked up, surprised to see us all watching him. He turned back to the bowl.

"I'm drawing a map," he replied tersely. "The symbols act as directions. They'll guide us as we travel."

I hadn't a clue what he was talking about, but I decided not to push it. When the cup was full, he moved to a table, emptying another substance in with his blood.

"This is ash," he explained before I could ask. "It's from a tree out in the garden—centuries old."

"What tree?" asked my brother.

"The one I think you saw in your vision," Draven replied, glancing up at Phoenix. "It belongs to the Daughters."

He mixed the ash and his blood together, and when he'd finished he looked back up at us.

"We will meet the Daughters in the mists that surround Eritopia. The mists can be deadly if you do not show enough caution," he warned. "When I tell you to, you need to all hold hands, to be connected to me at all times. Under no circumstances must you let go—do you understand?"

We all nodded silently.

"If you let go, you will be lost—doomed to forever wander in the mists between the rest of the In-Between and Eritopia, never existing in either space. The shape-shifters also inhabit the mists, though these are slightly different—more deadly than the ones Serena encountered in the swamp. They are shifters who have changed form too many times, and as a result have been driven mad, unable to reclaim their own identity. They will call to you, trying to separate you from one another. Pay them no attention. They can't harm you if we're together."

I felt sick. The thought of facing those shape-shifters, but in a deadlier state than the ones I'd already encountered, was terrifying.

"Don't worry," Draven replied, more softly, his gaze directed at me. "They can't harm you. I promise, I won't let anything happen to you."

I nodded. I trusted him.

Draven picked up the cup again, and moved over to the flame. It was the same, ever-burning fire that I had seen The Shade in. He placed the bowl in its center, the flame completely consuming it from sight.

"Connect to one another," he commanded, moving forward to take my hand. His skin was warm next to mine, his grip firm and reassuring. Bijarki joined the end of the 'line', taking Vita's hand. I was furious, but before I could complain, the room shifted and blurred in my vision, eventually melting away till all I could see was darkness, and gray, swirling mists.

PHOENIX

I closed my eyes against the mists, feeling a brief but intense suction-like sensation as if my entire body was being forced forward against my will. When I opened them again, we were all standing on cracked, red earth. Without letting my grip on Vita or Field go, I looked around, expecting to see evidence of a portal, but behind me there was nothing except a wide, empty expanse with nothing breaking up the line of the horizon. In front of us there was a large sandstorm barrier, following the earth in a straight line as far as I could see, and as tall as the plantation house so it was impossible to see what lay beyond it. The barrier whipped and screamed as the wind blew hot, grit-filled air in our faces.

"What is this place?" Field murmured.

I stared at the huge sandstorm in front of us, guessing that Draven would be telling us to walk through it, but wishing he wouldn't. I couldn't help but feel, though the barrier was only sand and wind, that it was furious—that it wanted to rip and tear and destroy anything that crossed its path.

"Remember what I told you!" Draven shouted out over the noise of the winds. "Whatever you do, don't let go."

He moved us forward, looking back to ensure the link hadn't been broken. Vita's grip was like a clamp, her eyes wide as we approached the wall.

"Don't worry," I murmured to her, thinking immediately what a stupid thing it was to say—there were *plenty* of reasons to be worried.

The sand slapped at my face like a whip, tearing at my hair and the loose shirts we'd been wearing from what the girls had managed to scavenge in the attic. It felt like my skin would blister from the onslaught—any exposed flesh felt like it was being burnt by both the intense heat and the grains of sand.

I lost sight of both Vita and Field. I looked down, squinting at where our hands were clasped, but I could only see their fingers and wrists—beyond that, they were swallowed by the barrier. Once we were inside the sandstorm, the ferocity of the wind had died down, so it no longer felt like it was roaring at us, but the density of the sand didn't let up. I soon felt I was completely lost and alone. No wonder Draven had told us to hang on tightly to one another—it felt like I could be lost in here forever, completely disorientated and never finding a way out.

We kept moving forward. I started to hear a strange whistling noise, as if it was coming from everywhere at once. I tried to tune into it, to listen more closely, beginning to distinguish strange voices and sounds.

"Can you hear that?" I called to Field and Vita.

"Yeah," Vita replied, her voice muffled, but Field didn't reply.

"Field?" I called, but he remained silent. I tugged on his arm, to get his attention. He tried to yank out of my grip but I held on tight.

"Field, are you okay?" I yelled again.

Silence.

I looked down at our hands, reassuring myself that he

was still there. Perhaps he couldn't hear me. There was nothing much else I could do other than make sure my grip didn't falter.

The whispered voices continued, and I stopped, stunned, as my name was called.

Phoenix.

Vita and Field both yanked me forward, and the voice was swallowed up by the cacophony of the other strange sounds and whistles carried in the winds. A few moments later, I could hear my name being called again, and it was in a voice I was sure I could recognize, but couldn't quite place.

Phoenix.

Why haven't you told your friends that you saw her?

I looked around, instantly angry. Who was this? Was it the Druid or Bijarki taunting me? Had they seen me trying to dig her up last night?

She is beautiful, isn't she?

But will you be worthy, Phoenix?

Are you a great man like your father—or are you a mere shadow of him?

I gritted my teeth against the voice. I was now sure it wasn't any of our company. I doubted the Druid or Bijarki knew anything of my father, or my relationship with him. How I truly felt. But someone was managing to push my buttons…Who? I listened out for the voice again, trying to rack my brain to work out where I'd heard it before.

"Don't listen to the voices!" Serena shouted across the winds. It snapped me back to reality. "Remember, the shape-shifters!"

Right. Yes, the creatures that had called out to my sister in the swamp, taking on the voices of Field and Jovi. The shape-shifters must have been mimicking the voice of one of us, but distorting it so it was unfamiliar and couldn't be placed.

Phoenix. The voice came again. *Phoenix.*

If you come with us, we will show you how to save her.

You can be with her, always.

You can find true love, contentment.

I yanked once again at the hands of my friends. Their grip was suddenly irritatingly tight. Why wouldn't they let me go? I wanted to follow the voices, let them lead me back to her, find a way to remove her from the worm-filled earth, from the rot and decay that surrounded her.

Come with us, Phoenix.

I looked around, searching the empty expanse of the

sandstorm. I could see shapes, emerging from the mists, but flickering so quickly in and out of my vision I wasn't sure if they were real or imagined. I squinted, trying to make them out.

One appeared in front of me, a few yards ahead. It was the figure of a man, I was sure of it, but from this distance, and with the sand still stinging unrelentingly in my eyes, I couldn't make out any particular features. The figure struck me as strange though, as if its arms were too long for its body, its head too slim and small for its frame. As I watched it, the figure flickered and darted away, moving at great speed.

"Wait!" I called out, trying to run after it.

"No!" Vita cried out. "Phoenix, don't listen to them! They're lying to us!" She pulled on my arm, keeping me alongside her. Field's grip didn't falter either.

I saw another, moving up ahead through the mists. It was running on all fours, not upright like a man, but still with a human figure—long legs that arched its spine upward, its arms scrabbling in the dirt while its face appeared to be turned at an unnatural angle, looking at me as it ran past. They moved *fast*—surprisingly so.

The noises started to give way to cries. Long, pain-filled

and tortured, they echoed through the winds. I knew my friends had been right to hold on tightly and not let me go. These creatures were hungry. I could hear their howls of misery that none of us would join them.

Help us! they now cried. *Please help us!*

The voices that called out were no longer familiar. They belonged to the tortured and insane—wretched creatures that seemed to be locked in these mists. Never finding their way home, only desiring to feed, to follow their most base instincts.

I shuddered, gripping Vita and Field tightly. I couldn't wait to get out of here. How long did this barrier continue on for? I couldn't see an end in sight, just more of the red and yellow hues of the sandstorm with the same dark, flickering figures lying in wait up ahead.

I dreaded the voices calling to me again, tempting me to follow them, using the girl as a ploy. Had the others heard what they'd been saying to me, or had they been locked in their own madness, the shape-shifters playing on their innermost secrets? My own behavior seemed completely baffling to me now, especially what I had done this morning. Why wasn't I telling my friends about the girl I'd seen? It was foolish, and actually downright dangerous, to keep them ignorant of what lay beneath the magnolia tree. It started to occur to me that the shape-shifters weren't the only ones that had managed to create some kind of hold over me—last night I had been scrabbling at the dirt with my bare hands in some kind of desperate frenzy to uncover her. Was the sleeping beauty manipulating me in some way? Using me to uncover something that was just an illusion, or something potentially deadly?

The Druid needed to be told of what I'd seen when I visited the tree—that I knew about the last Daughter's hiding place.

The tree had come from the Daughters of Eritopia, and if they were as dangerous as Bijarki and the Druid had claimed they could be, then I needed to be on guard. I vowed not to visit the magnolia tree again till I had told the others. It just wasn't safe.

Vita's hand pulled again suddenly on mine, and I gripped her more tightly.

"Focus on my voice," I called to her. "They're not real. Keep hold of me."

"Vita, no!" Bijarki yelled, at the same time that Vita tried to slide out of my grip. Our hands were becoming hot and slick with perspiration, making it harder to hold on to one another. I quickly grabbed her wrist as her fingers slipped from mine, holding on to her delicate bones, almost afraid that I could break them. I ignored my concerns—better an injured wrist than Vita breaking free and joining the shape-shifters.

Soon, her pulling stopped and it seemed like she'd come back to reality. Her arm went limp and the tension of my arm lessened as she moved closer next to me. I worried again that Field hadn't made a noise, but his grip was still firmly in mine.

Slowly, the whipping of the sand seemed to die down. I thought I could see a horizon beyond the storm—hope that we would soon be leaving the sand behind. Sure enough, a few minutes later, all of us picking up the pace in a desperate need to escape the creatures and their taunts, the sands died down completely. We stepped out on to the same cracked red earth, finally freed.

SERENA

I was relieved beyond words to finally escape the sandstorm. I had thought my experience in the swamp would have prepared me for facing the shape-shifters again—and in a way, it had—but their tactics were different this time, and far more insidious. At first, I had thought it was Draven calling to me, but then the voices had started speaking *about* Draven, and how, if I ever wanted to get home, to realize my dreams of Brown and the other Ivy League colleges I was so set on, I would need to leave him and my friends and follow them. I had found myself bizarrely tempted, even though I knew deep down what they were offering was completely illogical. They had also told me it was Draven himself who had brought about Elissa's death and his father's eventual downfall. None of this could have been true, but the shape-shifters did such a good job at painting Draven out as a cruel, vindictive demon that the moment we left the storm, I dropped his hand abruptly.

No one spoke for a few moments as we stood looking out at the horizon. The earth was the same as before—red and cracked, completely desolate, with arid sand brushing up against my bare feet as it was sucked into the storm behind us.

"That was intense," Jovi said huskily, not looking at any of us as he kicked the ground with his shoe. His tone was bitter, and I wondered what he had been told in there. Draven looked no better than the rest of us—his expression was pale and haunted, and he looked out on the horizon with his lips set in a disgusted grimace.

I was confused about where we were. From the way Draven had spoken, I had thought we'd be out in the atmosphere of the planets somewhere, staring at them all in the distance, in the same way we traveled through the In-Between from the portal to the fae star. If the Daughters were guardians of Eritopia, why were they on ground level?

Why were they on a star? I asked the Druid to explain, partly trying to distract him and refocus our guide on the matter in hand.

"This is all an illusion," he muttered. "None of it is real. Not the desert, the sandstorm—they're just protections created by the Daughters. I don't exactly know where we are."

"But our bodies are really here, right?" I asked, checking as I tried to gain an understanding of a land that was just illusion. "We're not just back in the basement, dreaming or anything?"

The Druid shook his head with a smirk.

"No, we're really here, it's just that 'here' doesn't exactly exist."

"Right," I replied sarcastically. That made zero sense.

"So, what do we do now?" Jovi asked. "Where do we find the Daughters?"

"We don't, they find us," Draven replied, moving over to a rock that jutted out from the earth—the only barrier I could see against the steady influx of sand that ran like an ocean along the earth. It provided a little shade from the intensity of the sun's glare, and I went to join him, already feeling like my skin was burning.

"For how long?" I asked as I sat down.

"As long as it takes," he replied, exhibiting a patience I didn't share in the slightest.

One by one my friends and brother sat down to join us. Bijarki was the only one who remained standing, pacing up and down as if he was unbothered by the heat of the day and preferred to remain active.

"This heat is intolerable," Aida grumbled, holding her hair up off the back of her neck. Her cheeks and nose were already growing pink, and both Jovi and Field shoved over to give her more space in the shade.

I started to look around in concern.

"Hang on. We have water, right?" I couldn't see any other way of getting it unless we'd brought it along, and neither Bijarki nor Draven looked like they had any provisions.

"We do," Draven replied.

I looked at him questioningly, and the others followed suit. Mentioning 'water' had been a mistake—my throat suddenly felt as dry as the land we were sitting on. Draven removed something from his pocket. He opened up his hand to reveal a small blue crystal. It glimmered in the light.

Right. Magic, of course.

I should have been used to stuff like this, having lived in The Shade, but as I didn't have any of the skills myself, I often assumed a rational state of mind, forgetting that others had access to a completely different kind of reality.

"What's that?" Vita asked, leaning over me and eyeing the crystal with curiosity.

"A form of the hemimorphite crystal," he replied. "It's known as a 'throat healer' in some Earth cultures, I believe."

He rolled the crystal along the ground and it came to a stop about two meters away from where we were sitting. I watched as the crystal started to morph, spreading out as if the earth was melting it, until it became a smooth pool of water. I was about to exclaim that it was unlikely to be enough for all of us when the water started to move more forcefully—a jet reaching up into the air and falling back down when it reached its apex, like a water fountain.

"How long will it last?" I asked, already getting up, transfixed by the cool, clear water.

"Long enough," Draven replied. "Just take your fill."

I greedily drank from the fountain, letting the water run down my chin and drench the front of my already sweat-soaked clothing. The others moved to stand behind me, everyone but Draven and the incubus forming an orderly queue for the water.

"Come on, Serena," my brother growled, "I'm dying here."

I took another gulp and stood aside, making my way back to the rock. I felt a million times better having drunk something, and started to wonder if the Druid had a way of getting us food as well.

"What's the longest time you've ever had to wait for them?" I asked, my impatient nature wanting to work out how long, roughly, we'd be stuck under the punishing heat.

"A day and a night," he replied.

Damn. This was going to be longer than I thought. I looked across the shelter of the rock into the distance, seeing if I could see anything that might be considered more suitable shelter, but there didn't seem to be much—a few rocks, but none much larger than this one.

I settled back down on the ground, resigned to our fate.

It didn't help matters that none of us wanted to talk much. It looked like everyone was still shell-shocked from their experience in the mists—some more than others. Field, I thought, must have had a particularly tough time of it—I'd never seen him look so shaken. Aida was the same. To make matters worse, we seemed particularly skittish around one another—Aida hadn't so much as glanced at Field since we emerged, and I jumped to the logical conclusion that the voices might have been taunting her about a seemingly unrequited love. I hoped not. I imagined that her situation was bad enough as it was, without her worst fears exposed by the shape-shifters.

Once we all reconvened back at the rock, Draven spoke.

"When the Daughters arrive, none of you say a word. Let me do the talking. Remember what I said about them. They are fickle and merciless, and even if you don't like what I'm saying, you are to remain silent."

His last words were directed at the incubus, who rolled his eyes.

"Trust me, I'm not in any hurry to talk to them," Bijarki replied emphatically. I wondered if he'd had dealings himself with the Daughters—was that why he'd been so reluctant before?

"Why not?" I asked, hoping he'd enlighten us.

"The Daughters aren't fans of my species," he replied, shrugging as if it didn't bother him much either way. "Long ago—we're talking centuries here, which will tell you a little bit about how long they can hold a grudge—one of the Daughters fell in love with an incubus. She foolishly renounced her guardianship of Eritopia to be with him. He didn't love her back, and left her to be with another woman of his own species—a succubus. The Daughter was purposeless and alone—she wouldn't be accepted back by the Daughters, they felt that their sister had betrayed them and wanted nothing more to do with her. She wandered the lands of the Eritopian galaxy till she died, some say of a broken heart. Dying is something that the Daughters aren't meant to be able to do, but somehow—whether it was because she was out of the fold of their protection and magic, I don't know—this one did. Hypocritically, the Daughters mourned her, and since then have even less love for our species than they do for the rest of the creatures in Eritopia."

"Why on earth did we bring him along, then?" I burst out, directing my question at Draven. The Druid laughed out loud.

"It makes no difference," he replied carelessly, "the Daughters will know already that Bijarki and I are working together. There is nothing, no secret or action, that can be hidden from them for long."

I sighed, leaning back against the rock. I still didn't think it was a good idea to have brought Bijarki along. It would hardly help our case, and his story made me even more wary of his species—though him specifically, and the designs he had on my friend. The incubus from the story had obviously somehow managed to trick the Daughter into believing that he loved her, otherwise who would face such a horrible fate? I wasn't surprised that they hated the incubi.

I glanced over at Vita, who had managed to become even paler than before. She was staring at the ground as if deep in thought, and I wondered if she too was thinking about the dangerous nature of the species. I hoped she was. Bijarki couldn't be trusted.

"I'm going for a walk," I stated, getting up off the floor to stretch my legs. The heat was bad, but I'd go crazy sitting there all day. Vita and Aida both scrambled to their feet.

"We'll come with you," Aida said, looking relieved to get away.

"Don't go far," Draven warned. "We are in uncharted territory."

I nodded dully, already feeling drowsy as the heat beat down on my scalp. Bijarki cast a look in Vita's direction, as if angling for an invitation. I scowled at him, and he averted his eyes.

Don't even think about it.

When would Bijarki get the hint that I'd rather pummel him to a bloody pulp than let him get anywhere near my friend? I'd give him some credit—he certainly had thick skin and persistence. But like the incubus in the story, I doubted that his ardor would last.

SERENA

We'd walked around for a short while, looking at the nothingness of the dry and desolate land, none of us really speaking. I'd tried to get Vita and Aida to open up about what the shape-shifters had called out to them, but neither of them seemed willing to share. I understood that. I imagined that my particular fears were small fry compared to both girls'. I doubted any of us really knew the full extent of what they'd seen in their visions, how horrific it had been to be up close with the Destroyers or speaking to the Oracle.

What worried me most was that this would be the start of a separation between the three of us, a void in our friendships that wouldn't ever fully recover. We'd always been so close, and had shared most things. Would that be lost now? Would the experience of Eritopia create an unfixable separation? I hoped not. The tough situations we were facing, at least in my mind, should have been bringing us closer together, not further apart. It was the same with my brother—he had always been a bit aloof, never letting me in on what he got up to in Hawaii, but other than that we'd been close. We'd shared a lot and helped one another as much as we could at home—small things, like homework, household chores, etc., but that stuff had mattered, and we had a sibling bond that was pretty solid by ordinary standards.

Once the novelty of walking had worn off, all three of us made our way back to the rock, desperate for more water. The sky had started to darken to the west, and I imagined it would be nightfall before long. I'd heard how cold deserts could get in the evening, and I wondered if this would be the case here.

When we returned, Draven had lit a fire—it seemed to appear from the core of the earth, as there were no branches or any kind of wood that could have created it. But the flame was strong, heat radiating off it, and smoke billowing up into the air.

"Is this the same flame that's in the basement?" I asked curiously. It might have been nice to take a look at The Shade for a while. Even if it was painful, I'd have loved to see my parents' faces just for a few moments, to reassure myself they were okay.

"No," Draven replied. "It's just a flame. Nothing can be seen. I'm sorry."

He had guessed my intentions, and his gaze met mine with pity in his eyes. I shrugged, pretending it didn't matter, and sat back against the rock.

Watching the fire, I started to grow drowsy. Draven had come to sit next to me, heat radiating off his body and warming me further. A breeze had picked up, and it lightly ruffled his hair, brushing it against his jawline. He seemed content to sit and watch the flames in silence, but when I looked down at his forearms I could see that his muscles seemed to be taut—as if he was coiled to spring into action at a moment's notice. Perhaps not as relaxed as I'd assumed, then.

As my body yearned for sleep and I tried to fight it, I felt an urge to lean my head on his broad shoulders—to close my eyes and lie against him in comfort, feeling the warmth of his skin through his shirt. I pinched myself on the back of my hand, trying to stay awake. It would *not* be comfortable to lean against the Druid—it would be downright weird.

Without warning, the flame stuttered and went out.

"They're coming," Draven whispered, standing. The rest of us followed his lead, all jolting out of our drowsy stillness. My heart began to race, half terrified at what was heading our way.

Draven reached down and gently squeezed my hand. I squeezed it back slightly, grateful for the gesture, then drew away. His face didn't betray any reaction to me, he just stared ahead, waiting for the Daughters to arrive.

They came at once, seven women suddenly appearing out of thin air. I held my breath, stunned first and foremost at their awe-inspiring and yet violent beauty. Their skin looked like it was painted in gold, and they were dressed in linens, the material wrapped and draped like Grecian goddesses'. Their hair was long and wild, some of it braided in intricate fashions, entwined with gold beads and jewels. Around their ankles, necks and arms they wore more gold, chains and amulets, large stones held together with long ropes of gold chain that looked as if they were impossibly heavy. Their faces were entirely covered by golden masks, and only their eyes could be seen, peering out at us, each of them a startling, violet-purple color I'd never seen on any other being before, supernatural or otherwise.

One of them stepped forward, breaking the line. She had brilliant red and orange hair—the color of flames or a sunset. It trailed down her back, and as the breeze continued to move over us, her hair wrapped itself around her arms, giving the impression that it had a life of its own. These women didn't look like supernatural creatures to me—they looked like goddesses, completely removed from the earth and anything concretely real.

"Druid, why have you disturbed us? We have helped you already, enough for many lifetimes. Do you think the Daughters of Eritopia are at your service?" Her voice was deep, resonating around us so that I could hear the hum of her voice in my veins long after she finished the last word.

I heard Draven exhale a low breath beside me, and then he bowed.

"Forgive us. We were sent by an Oracle. She told us to visit you. My home may no longer be safe, and the boy"— he gestured toward Phoenix—"has had a vision of the tree and the egg."

"Are you sure?" the redhead asked. The rest of the Daughters didn't move, but something had changed. There was now a perceptible tension in the air, as if the rest of them held their breath. This news obviously was important—but *what* was important to the Daughters about my Oracle brother having these visions, I didn't understand... Wasn't he supposed to only see the past, anyway? How could they find that so significant?

"I am sure," Draven replied.

Simultaneously, all of them, in one motion, turned to face my brother. They stood in silence, watching him with their strange eyes. My brother swallowed, looking deeply uncomfortable.

After a while, the redhead turned back to Draven.

"The Oracle was *wrong* to send you here," she said. "We can do nothing for you, and we will do nothing for you, until the last Daughter of Eritopia rises. She alone will help you end the reign of Azazel."

"It will be too late!" Draven retorted angrily.

I drew in sharply, worried that he'd raised his voice—I doubted it would take much to rile these women up—but they started to laugh.

"Then you will have failed," they replied in unison.

"But that is not our concern," the redhead continued. "We have already done what you asked of us. And you were warned then not to return."

"I have paid the price, and continue to pay the price for your help," Draven countered, his tone becoming clipped and angry. "The last Daughter is safe and remains safe! So long as you help us!"

"But I wonder for how long she will remain undisturbed?" This time the voice didn't come from the redhead, but from one of the other Daughters. Another stepped forward, moving toward Phoenix. She had black hair, almost reaching the floor. Small braids covered it from the center of her parting, each adorned with a thin chain and bright blue stones inlaid into the gold at various intervals.

My brother didn't move, but the Daughter reached out her hand and ran one finger down his cheek. Phoenix gasped, clutching the skin where she'd just touched him as if in pain.

"If you're going to remain unhelpful, then we will leave," Draven growled. The black-haired Daughter turned to him. Immediately all the Daughters looked hostile. I shrank back, wishing that the Druid had been more polite, but at the same time I wondered if his outburst had been to distract the black-haired Daughter from my brother.

"You forget, Druid, there is still a price for calling on us," the redhead replied, her voice tinged with amusement. My body felt cold all of a sudden. The request sounded like a threat. I had thought the price had already been paid with the Druid carving runes onto his body…would the Daughters now demand something of him too? I glanced over at Draven. The muscle in his jaw flickered, but he remained silent.

What price?

SERENA

Despite Draven's warnings, I wanted to say something to the Daughters, to know what price they felt he should pay. They had been next to useless—why would he have to give them anything?

"You have offered us nothing," Draven spat, clearly unable to hold his tongue any more than I could.

"You knew there would be a cost," the redhead replied. I felt Draven starting to tremble next to me. I knew it was through rage, not fear, and I worried about what he would do next. I didn't want him to incur their wrath any further than we already had done, and mentally begged for him to stay silent.

Draven didn't reply, and the Daughters stood there in silence, watching him. I glanced over at the others—none of them had taken their eyes off the Daughters, it was Bijarki alone who steadfastly looked at the floor. His fists were balled at his sides, his usually handsome face distorted by an expression of blind fury—or dread, I couldn't tell which.

The silence seemed to stretch on forever. Were they deliberating the price? Using a form of telepathy to confer amongst themselves? Or was it the redhead who would make the decision? I started to think that perhaps the price wasn't going to be too severe. Draven had mentioned the last Daughter he still guarded—well, looking after an object didn't seem that high a price to pay, even if the Daughters had been useless. I tried to focus on relaxing my muscles, trying to breathe and calm myself before I snapped.

"Payment has been decided," the redhead intoned, breaking the silence. I exhaled, relieved that the wait was over. "Considering that your actions were for a greater cause than your own selfish end, and for the good of Eritopia, we have decided to take a temporary gift—to be returned to you once we consider your debt to be repaid."

I looked over at Draven in relief. Surely this was good news? But the Druid hadn't moved, his steely gray eyes watching them carefully. He made no indication that he was relieved to hear about the temporary payment.

"Druid," the redhead continued, "you rely so heavily on the visions of those with the sight, much like the Destroyers you profess to hate. Thus, we have decided that we will take your own vision. Perhaps afterward, you will learn to trust and value your own sense when it is returned to you. Let it be a lesson, and let our benevolence remind you of our greatness."

What?

I didn't have long to wonder. Draven cried out in unspeakable pain, falling to his knees, as the Daughters laughed. I crouched down next to him in a panic, not knowing what to do. The black shutters I had seen before when Field had tried to attack him came over his eyes. Then blood started to pour out of his sockets.

"STOP!" I screamed, ignoring the Druid's earlier warning. How could they do this to him? When I looked back up, the Daughters had vanished completely. Draven's cries stopped, and he collapsed further onto the floor, unconscious. The blood continued to seep out from behind the black veil over his sockets.

I ripped the hem of my dress, creating a bandage that I proceeded to wrap around his head. Bijarki helped me lift the back of his head up, and we tied it in a knot at his temple. Within moments, where the bandage covered his eyes, two crimson spots appeared and slowly spread outward.

"How do we stop the bleeding?" I asked the incubus.

He shook his head. "I think we have to wait till it's over. Can you try to syphon some of the pain away? We need to wake him," Bijarki replied.

Without bothering to reply, I pressed both my hands against Draven's chest. I sent my energy outward, locating his pain and trying to suck it out. Luckily, because it pertained mostly to the head, his pain was easy to find, but it was like red-hot coals, and my own energy seemed to wither and recede when I tried to hold onto it. I kept trying, unwilling to give up.

"Phoenix, help me!" I cried, calling my brother over. He came quickly, slamming his knees into the earth next to me. His hands joined mine on the Druid's chest, and soon I felt his energy, bright and golden, next to mine as we tried to remove some of the pain. With both our energies combined, it eventually started working. I could feel myself growing weaker as Draven's own pain polluted my mind, sending a dull ache to my temples.

But it worked. Draven inhaled sharply, taking in a lungful of air. He fought to sit up, but Bijarki and Phoenix both held him down.

"No, don't move," Bijarki instructed him, "lie still for now. You'll only make the pain worse."

The bleeding seemed to have stopped, but it didn't seem to mean much. The Druid would be blind—God knew for how long. Bijarki muttered profanities under his breath, cursing the Daughters relentlessly while the rest of us remained silent, too stunned to say a word. Draven's breathing stopped sounding so labored, and he waved my brother and Bijarki away.

"Leave me," he snarled. "I'm all right."

"No, you're not!" I exploded. "None of this is all right. We should never have come here. I'm so sorry."

I wanted to scrape off my own skin, I felt so wretched. I had persuaded Draven to come here, kept at him, no matter how many times he and Bijarki had warned me of the danger.

"It's not your fault," Draven replied quietly. "I chose to

come here. And no matter what has been done, we were right to try—the Oracle asked us to."

I shook my head in disagreement. We had not been right to try. This had been a stupid, reckless mission.

"We need to get out of here," Draven continued.

"No, you need to rest," Bijarki replied firmly. Draven grabbed for his arm, finding the material of his shirt and pulled him closer.

"Do as I *say*," he bit out. "We can't remain here. There's a stone in my pocket. Re-carve the runes."

Bijarki averted his eyes so I couldn't see his expression. He took the stone out, and held it in his hand.

"Please, Draven," he said. "Don't make me do this. Let's wait. You're in enough pain."

"Do it," Draven replied, his teeth clenched.

With a trembling hand, Bijarki parted his friend's shirt. The runes from earlier were still plainly visible—the blood had dried, but the carved skin was red and puckered. It looked painful, and I knew that if Bijarki were to go over them again, whatever pain the Druid currently felt would be doubled.

"We can stay," I said hastily. "It doesn't matter. Why not just go back tomorrow?"

Draven shook his head.

"We leave now. I don't want to take the risk. We need to get back to the house. Unless, of course, you want the Daughters to return and inflict more of their benevolence on us?"

"Do it," I said to Bijarki.

I reached for Draven's hand. I held him tightly, trying to offer the small amount of comfort that I could. Bijarki cut into his flesh again, holding on to his other arm to stop him shaking. I felt the smallest flicker of pity for the incubus. I wouldn't have liked to be in his place. I imagined that he felt every cut he made almost as keenly as the Druid did.

Draven only hissed as Bijarki got to work. I could barely look, and it wasn't long before my eyes started to fill with tears and blur, thankfully restricting my vision.

I would have given anything to turn back time in that moment. Had I understood the consequences, I would never have opened my big mouth. Damn the Daughters to hell—they might have been beautiful, but that couldn't hide the fact that they were the most wretched, despicable creatures I'd come across in both the natural and supernatural world.

Vita

Bijarki and Serena helped the Druid stagger to his feet. Blood ran off him, from his chest and eyes, staining him a brilliant red and matting the front strands of his golden-brown hair.

"Take it easy," murmured Bijarki as Draven tried to stand on his own. Bijarki and Serena stood either side of him, supporting him as best they could, their arms tucked under his and flung over his back.

"All of you make a connection," the Druid instructed hoarsely.

We hurried to do his bidding. Bijarki took my hand

again, and though my first reaction was to yank it back and move to where Aida or Jovi were, I didn't want to cause unnecessary fuss. I held on tight, knowing what would be heading our way when we reached the mists. Aida came and stood on the other side of me, clasping my hand and taking Phoenix's with the other.

Once we were all linked, we started to move toward the sandstorm. I dreaded re-entering it, hearing the voices again with their horrible calls that seemed to penetrate to the truth of my soul—secrets I kept hidden suddenly exposed in a way that made me feel violated and bare, as if they could peer inside my head and heart.

We stepped inside the storm, and like last time, visibility became nil as the hot sands whipped at our faces. It no longer felt like dusk. In the middle of the storm it was impossible to tell what time of day it was or what direction we were heading in.

"Remember not to listen to the voices!" Serena called out. Aida's hand tightened on mine in reassurance, and, I suspected, fear.

We kept moving. It wasn't long till the strange whistles started up. I had thought about those noises when we'd entered the desert. I hadn't understood what they were before, but now I thought that the noises were calls—the shape-shifters letting others know that their prey was near.

This time I saw the flickering movements of the creatures before I heard them calling. They ran in and out of the billows of sand, sometimes moving on two legs and making their appearance more human, other times on all fours like emaciated beasts, their spines arched backward and their long hind legs making them look hideously unnatural and perverted.

Vita.

I heard them call my name, and I tried to shut them out, thinking of other things, anything to keep their voices at bay. I started to list, alphabetically, the herbs and plants that Zerus had taught me. I recited a rhyme that my mom used to sing to me as a kid…Anything and everything—my mind jumping from one subject to the next in a panic to keep their calls at bay.

Vita.

Do you still want him now?

After the story you heard?

Why do you even think he told it? Was it a warning to you?

I held Aida's hand tightly. I could feel her trembling, or perhaps it was me, I couldn't tell. The sands whipped at my face and hair. I shut my eyes, trying not to see anything as I moved one foot in front of the other with painstaking slowness.

I could hear them laughing. It was a cruel, cold sound—twisted laughter that bore so little resemblance to the real thing that it sounded more like screams of pain. I shuddered, returning to the rhyme, returning to images of The Shade—the redwood trees in autumn, the lake when it was frosted at the edges, the lighthouse, the sea in summer and the foam of the waves as they hit the shore. Images of my mom laughing, the broad smile of my dad, Zerus talking softly to himself as he moved through the forests, touching the bark of a tree, caressing a leaf and telling it how well it was growing.

You'll end up like that Daughter of Eritopia, Vita... lost and alone, wandering the land with a hollow and dead heart...waiting for him to love you.

He never will, Vita, a mouse like you? No, you'll never be loved. It will elude you, like the control over your own elements...a useless semi-fae, with barely enough power to light a match.

"No!" Aida cried out, yanking on my arm. I held on tight, helping her fight her own demons while I simultaneously battled with my own.

Nobody notices you, the voices whispered—closer this time, as if they were drawing in.

Come with us.

We would never dismiss you, we would love you.

This time I sighed with relief. If they were calling to me to come with them, it was almost over. I just needed to overcome the final call—the pull on my heart that was meant to make me want to break the chain. Perhaps it was because it was the second time, and I knew all too well what their aim was, and knew I wasn't alone in this—all my friends were battling the same cries, the same secrets being used against them to cause pain—that I managed to hang on to Aida and Bijarki.

His grip had remained firm and consistent throughout the journey, never once trying to yank away. When he felt my grip falter, despite my best efforts, he held on tighter.

Slowly the storm started to grow sparser, and we stepped out from the barrier. I took in a lungful of air, finally able to breathe freely. Without thinking, I tried to drop both Aida and Bijarki's hands.

"Not yet," Bijarki reminded me.

Hastily I tightened my grip, recalling the last step of

travel required us to remain linked to one another. I looked around me, barely able to make out a single feature of the desert in the gloom of dusk, and in the very next moment I felt a sickening jolt in my stomach, as if my internal organs were being pulled down inside of me. I closed my eyes, grimacing at the unpleasant sensation. When I opened them again, we were standing back in the laboratory room of the plantation house. For once, I was pleased to be there.

Bijarki instantly released my hand, turning to Draven. He helped the Druid down onto the stone floor, yanking an old rag from one of the tables to place beneath his head.

"What can we do?" Serena asked Draven, looking around in vain as if she might recognize some of the strange liquids and herbs.

"I need *Agrimonia*," Draven replied, his voice barely above a whisper now. "*Pelargonium, Vinca minor, Thuja* oil."

Bijarki and Serena looked at one another with panicked confusion, but as he listed the herbs I realized I recognized a few of the names. Some were earthly ingredients.

"Okay," I said, rushing over to the shelves where rows and rows of glass jars contained a myriad of different herbs and leaves. "I think I know this!"

I searched the shelf. I found the *Agrimonia* easily—Zerus had made me study it, and we had a small bush of it in my garden by the Sanctuary. I took the jar and emptied the contents on the table top. I rushed back to the shelves, looking for *Vinca minor*—another of the herbs that I recognized. I found it, and emptied the jar next to *Agrimonia*.

"Draven," I said crouching down next to him, "can you describe *Pelargonium* to me? I don't know it!"

"Geranium," he replied with a faint smile.

Stupid me. Of course I knew it—he had used the Latin name, that was all. I found the jar quickly, and then asked about the *Thuja* oil.

"Bottom shelf," Draven rasped. "Yellow oil. Mix it all together, and heat it. Becomes a paste. Put…put it on the wounds."

His voice was growing fainter. I checked the bottom shelf, panic making it difficult for me to focus. There seemed to be more than one yellow jar on the shelf. Typically, like the rest of the ingredients, nothing was labeled. I picked up the three yellowish jars of liquid. I moved them about. Only one of them had the consistency of oil—the rest were like water. I grabbed the jar and took it back to the table.

"What can I do to help?" Bijarki asked me, appearing at my side.

"I need something to boil this in," I replied. Everyone jumped to action. A few moments later, various pots and iron cauldrons were placed in front of me. I took the sturdiest-looking and moved it over to one of the makeshift stoves that were built into the table. It had a container of oil at the base, and a thick, fabric wick. A very basic ring of iron was arranged over it, creating the stove surface. I placed the cauldron on top and started to add the herbs, crushing them down with a pestle. Next I added the oil and lit the wick.

"Can I help?" Field asked.

I shook my head, concentrating on the liquid. I wanted to make sure I took the heat away at exactly the right moment. I knew from experience that if I left it too long the paste would return to liquid, and I'd have to start all over again.

When it was at the right consistency, I cut the heat and removed the cauldron from the stove using a rag to protect my hands. I carried it over to the Druid.

"How do we get it on the wounds?" I asked. Draven didn't reply.

"Draven?" Serena called his name sharply, applying pressure to his arm. He groaned, looking as if he was about to pass out again.

She looked at me worriedly, and then scooped out the paste with her fingers.

"Serena!" I gasped, worried it might be hot.

"It's okay," she replied. Very carefully, she started to apply the paste to the runes.

"Let me do that," I said gently, scooping out the paste. "You do his eyes."

She nodded, tentatively removing the bandage from around his head. I heard her inhale sharply as she looked at the bloodied eye-sockets of the Druid.

"Bijarki," I added, "get something to clean them with first."

He nodded, moving off to one of the tables. I tried not to look at Draven's face. This was all my fault. If I hadn't had that stupid vision, none of this would have happened, and if Serena and I hadn't insisted that we should visit the Daughters, Draven would still have his sight.

A second later, Bijarki was back. With a surprising amount of tenderness and care, he wiped away the blood around Draven's eyes using a damp cloth that smelt strongly of alcohol. Before the bleeding could begin again, Serena applied the paste—her focus and professional manner were impressive. I didn't consider myself particularly squeamish, but I thought I might have found it difficult if our roles had been swapped.

Once I'd finished on the runes, Draven's breathing started to sound more robust.

"Thank you," he murmured.

"I'll get some water," I muttered to Serena, noticing his dry lips. I ran the faucet from a work sink in the corner of the room and found a glass.

"What about your eyesight?" Serena asked.

"Just have to wait," Draven breathed.

I hurried over with the water. Serena took the glass from me, and lifted his head so that he could drink. He took two small sips and nodded, waving the water away.

"I'm fine now," he muttered. "I just need to lie down."

"I'll take you to your room," Serena replied. She looked up at Bijarki, indicating that he should help the Druid stand. Together they lifted him up. Once again, Draven made little to no indication as to whether or not he was in pain—only a sharp intake of breath and a short hiss of discomfort was uttered as he stood.

"I've got this," Serena told Bijarki.

He nodded, letting her take the weight of Draven's body as the two of them walked toward the main section of the basement and up the stairs.

"Are you sure you're all right?" Jovi asked as Serena staggered past him.

"I'm fine, honestly," Serena replied.

She was determined to help. I wondered how much of that was guilt—we had both been urging Draven to see the Daughters, and Serena wouldn't be taking the consequences lightly. But there was something else too. Serena and Draven had established a bond—whether it was only friendship or something else, I didn't know. What I did know was that whether she was fascinated by him or furious with him, Draven always managed to elicit a reaction from her, effortlessly consuming her focus. I didn't yet know if that was a good or bad thing.

When Serena and Draven left, the others started to follow them, all of us eager to get out of the basement.

"Are you coming?" Aida asked.

"I just need to clear this stuff," I replied, re-stocking the herbs I hadn't used.

"I'll help," she replied. I looked up at my friend's pale

and pinched face. The journey had been particularly hard on her, on both the way in and out.

"No, get some rest," I replied, meaning it. Aida looked like she needed to sleep for a week. I felt the same, but my mind was too hyper to rest. It was buzzing from the interaction with the Daughters, and the whispers of the sandstorm.

"Thanks." She nodded, turning to leave. Her shoulders were slumped, her back stooped in a slouch—something I hadn't seen her do since we were in our early teens. Whatever the shape-shifters had told Aida, it wasn't good.

I continued to preoccupy myself by putting the herbs back in order, tempted to start labeling the ones I recognized on the shelf, but holding myself back, doubting that Draven would appreciate my interference.

"He should clean up in here more."

I jumped at the sound of Bijarki's voice. I hadn't realized that I still had company.

"He should," I agreed, mumbling my words. I hadn't wanted to be left alone with Bijarki, especially not after the taunting of the shape-shifters, the vision I'd had of us in the valley, and on top of that, yesterday, I'd had a very strange, very disturbing dream about him. As far as Bijarki was concerned, I wanted him to stay as far away from me as possible.

"Can I do anything to help?" he offered. I heard him move toward me, crossing the room with even steps that echoed in the now empty laboratory.

"No," I managed, shoving the last of the dried herbs in a jar.

"You look beautiful when you're nervous. Your heart rate increases dramatically, and you flush the palest pink on your cheeks." His voice was smooth and soft, almost becoming a caress as the words dripped from his mouth.

"What?" I replied, doing my best to sound indignant.

"It's just an observation," he replied gently. He was moving closer. I could feel his body behind me, moving into my personal space—not touching me, but so determinedly *there* that I couldn't ignore it.

"Well, don't," I replied, anxiety coursing through me. "I don't want your observations. I want you to leave me alone. Stop staring at me, looking at me like you *know* me. You don't."

I wasn't sure where I'd gotten the courage to say all that to his face, but when I'd finished my small Vita-sized tirade, I was glad. I had stuck up for myself—put up boundaries.

"I'm sorry," he replied. The voice was less self-assuredly smooth this time.

"It's fine," I replied curtly. "Just don't do it anymore. It makes me uncomfortable."

He vanished from my personal space, moving back across the room. With some distance between us, I felt free to glance over at him. He looked despondent and conflicted, his eyes glued to the floor. He reached up and scratched the back of his neck.

"It just…" He hesitated, "It comes naturally with you— it's incredibly hard to be any other way. But I apologize… I will stay away."

I wasn't sure exactly what he meant by "it", but I hoped this would be the end of whatever he had going on—that my dreams and visions would be incubus-free going forward. As he left the room, I turned back to the mess on the table… and wondered why *I* suddenly felt despondent.

SERENA

I helped Draven back to his room. I staggered under his weight, half-wishing I'd accepted Jovi's offer of help, but I felt like I should take the weight of this responsibility—literally. With every hitched breath Draven took, my feelings of guilt worsened. I stayed silent though, focusing on putting one foot in front of the other like I'd done in the sandstorm, putting all my energy into getting him to his bedroom before I collapsed under his weight.

Clearly, a visit to the Daughters wouldn't be repeated any time soon, and I hoped for all our sakes that they stayed as far away from us as possible. I didn't know why the

Oracle had sent us to them. We had thought that she was a 'fairy godmother'... what a joke. I didn't know if her instructions to Vita had been malevolent, but so far her 'gifts' and advice had landed us in deeper and deeper trouble. Anything else she passed along to us from now on would be taken with a grain of salt. I just wasn't sure we could continue to trust her. She was Azazel's creature now. Draven had said that visions could be interfered with...we had to consider the possibility that what the Oracle had said to us so far had been distorted by him. It was a sobering thought.

We reached the door, and I pushed it open. I glanced at Draven, his chiseled jaw clenched with the effort of not verbally expressing his pain. I laid him on the bed as gently as I could, and he muttered his thanks.

"Don't thank me," I replied. "You knew it was dangerous and I didn't listen."

He appeared too distracted by the pain to respond—just sank his head against his pillow with a grunt.

The fire was roaring in his bedroom—somehow it had managed to stay burning since we'd left—and I wished it would burn itself out. The heat in the room was stifling. I looked around for a jug of water, and found one—grossly lukewarm, but it would have to do. I poured the water in a cup next to it, and carried it over to him.

"Here," I said, taking his hand and placing the cup in it. "Drink."

He took a few sips, and then waved the cup away. I placed it down by the edge of the bed, and arranged the cushions under his head.

"Stop fussing," he growled.

I stopped.

"Is there anything you need?" I asked.

"No."

I sat myself down at the edge of the bed, planning to stay till he fell asleep.

"Let me just take off your boots," I added. "Get you more comfortable."

"I can do it," he breathed. He tried to move himself into a sitting position, but winced, clutching his head as he did so.

"Let me," I insisted, frustrated that he was such a terrible patient. He would do himself more damage if he didn't relax. I removed his shoes, dropping them onto the floor.

"Can I syphon more of your pain?" I asked.

"I'm fine. My head hurts, that's all."

"Yeah, because you've had your eyeballs removed," I retorted. "Just let me help, okay?"

"If you're going to stay here just sit quietly."

I sighed, relenting. "Fine," I said, though I wasn't sure how long I'd be able to sit in silence. It wasn't exactly a skill of mine. He seemed to relax at my acceptance, the tension draining from his body as he sank into the mattress.

His chest was bare, Bijarki having removed his shirt once the runes were re-drawn. Even bloodied and scarred the way he was, and covered with the healing paste, there was an undeniable beauty to his body. The ripples of muscle across his chest and torso gently moved as he drew ragged breaths, but where his skin was untouched, it appeared tanned and smooth. I shook my head, looking away.

What are you doing?

I moved to sit in the armchair by the bed, easing myself off the mattress carefully so as to not disturb him. From this angle, I could see his profile more clearly—his face had lost the tense contortions of his pain, and his eye sockets had stopped bleeding. I wondered how long it would be before the Daughters gave him his sight back. Hopefully not too long. We needed him now, more than ever.

"Serena," he murmured, breaking the silence.

"Yes?"

"It's now vital that you don't leave the confines of the house and garden. You need to stay extra vigilant—promise me that. I can't protect you like this."

"I promise," I replied, honestly. "I'm capable of looking after myself, and I have the others too. We won't let anything happen—we'll stay safe."

"I don't trust you, or anyone else, to protect yourself," he whispered, and I wondered if he'd become delirious. His voice did have a spacey dream-like quality that made me think it was likely. Perhaps it was the paste we'd applied to his skin taking effect—doing more than just stemming the bleeding.

"You need to start," I responded. "I'm not fragile—what happened with the shape-shifters on my first night won't happen again. I've learned my lesson."

Draven shook his head. He emitted a low, rasping laughter.

"You think you can depend entirely on yourself," he replied. "You're delusional. You need me. You're just too stubborn to see it."

I smiled in amusement. Draven's words were beginning to slur—he was definitely delusional. A small flicker of temptation unfurled in my mind. He was weak right now. I could finally mind-meld with him without him noticing, or being able to do much about it. But it was just a thought. I knew I wouldn't act on it. I couldn't abuse his trust that way. After all he'd done for us, I needed to start considering him as an ally, if not a friend. My rule with syphoning was that I only did it with explicit permission from those I knew and trusted. Draven would now be counted as someone I trusted—even if I still knew very little about him. I decided I would leave him to get some sleep—if his filter was currently off, then it was probably better that I wasn't around.

I stood up, moving toward the door.

"Wait," he said hoarsely.

I turned abruptly, an eyebrow raised. "Yes?"

"Stay," he whispered.

A span of silence fell between us. "Uh, okay," I replied, even as I frowned at his request. His delirium was certainly causing him to act out of character. Only recently he'd snapped at me for watching him while he slept.

I quietly resumed my position in the armchair, and watched as he began to doze off. My eyes wandered along the contours of his tall body, then rested on his exhausted, handsome face.

I tried not to think about what he'd said regarding how I 'needed' him... I wasn't sure in what context that comment was meant—was it about protection, or something else?

As his breathing became deeper, steadier, I must have briefly given in to sleep too, because I woke to the sound of him groaning—trying to move the bandage that had been reapplied to his eyes as he slept. I quickly moved to the bed.

"Draven, it's okay," I breathed, trying to soothe him as I clutched his hands and set them down by his sides. It was difficult to do, he had much more strength than me, but in his sleeping state it was manageable, and eventually his groans gave way to regular breathing again.

Trying not to wake him, I placed my hands on his bare chest, reaching out with my mind to syphon away more of his pain. I again felt the urge to mind-meld with him, to see into his dreams, but I held back. Instead, I located the violent shards of red that seemed to be piercing into his temples, and gently took them on as my own pain. My body trembled with the effort—it was too soon since I'd done this last—but I persevered. I deserved to take some of the burden.

He didn't wake, and after a few moments, I removed my hands. I bent double over the mattress, my head pounding and my eyes wet with unshed tears caused by the smarting of pain.

It seemed like it was getting more painful each time. But watching Draven suffer alone was worse. Once again, I felt the magnitude of what he had done for us, all he had sacrificed, and not just for us—but for the good of his homeland and the creatures in it that he was so cut off from. I couldn't help but admire him for putting himself in danger like that. He had comfort and safety here, and while it might not have been perfect, I was pretty sure that most creatures in his position would just accept their fate—stay secluded here, and let the rest of Eritopia fall to the reign of Azazel.

When my temples had stopped pounding, I looked over at Draven. His face, glistening with tiny beads of perspiration, was lit by the fire that still burned in the hearth.

I let out a breath. There was so much I still didn't know about the Druid and the rest of his kind—what had happened to Elissa for her to have left this place, and what Draven was doing in keeping a mission that was looking increasingly hopeless going.

Like the mysterious new world that surrounded us, clearly there was more to this young man and his life story than he'd let on… A lot more.

My core instincts told me that if there was a key to our escape, Draven was it, but only if I unraveled him. He needed to start trusting me, truly—but for that to happen, I had to pull down some of my own barriers and attempt to get closer to him…

Draven stirred, his sheets slipping down his torso to an uncomfortably low area of his waist. I swallowed.

I just had to be careful not to entangle myself in the process.

PHOENIX

The moment we left the basement and entered the living room, I took Field, Jovi and Aida aside.

"I need to show you something," I muttered.

"Can't it wait?" Aida pleaded, her face drawn and pale.

"It can't, sorry," I replied curtly, but I meant it. I knew she needed to rest, but they also needed to know about the tree and the Daughter lying beneath it. Not just because I needed to unburden myself, but also because they needed to know—the information was obviously important, and I didn't trust myself to wait any longer. If I waited till tomorrow, I could see myself changing my mind, returning to the tree on my own and falling back under the spell of her beauty.

They dutifully followed me outside, and I took them round the side of the house to the entrance garden. The night was still and quiet, the moon so large in the sky that it gave us enough light to see by without the use of a lantern. In the darkness, the blossoms of the magnolia tree glistened like silver, and the moon's rays seemed to fall directly on the boughs like a spotlight.

"This is the tree I saw in the vision," I said, the words tumbling out before I could change my mind. "Beneath it lies the shell I saw as well, and inside that there's a girl—the last Daughter of Eritopia. She's just as beautiful as the others… more so. She's fast asleep—or in some kind of magic coma, I don't know."

All three of them stared down at the soil in silence. It occurred to me that they might not believe me. It wasn't like they could see what I saw.

"Why didn't you tell us before?" Field asked.

I looked guiltily in his direction.

"I'm sorry," I muttered. "I came here…She was so beautiful—so fragile, I suppose…She drew me in, and I just couldn't bear to tell anyone about it. I wanted to, but…

there was something stopping me. I'm sorry, Field. I know you asked, and I lied. Forgive me."

"It's okay," he replied, his voice without reproach. "I get it. The Daughters today—they were...Well." He cleared his throat. "Just be careful. That kind of beauty, it can be deadly."

"I know," I replied.

"Do you think we should dig her up?" Jovi asked, placing his hands down on the soil, testing its firmness.

"I don't think so," Field replied quickly. "We should wait to see what Draven thinks. Digging her up could be dangerous—we could harm her, or ourselves. I'm not particularly keen to incur the wrath of the Daughters again."

"I agree," Aida replied. "She's probably meant to be left alone—maybe that's one reason Draven was cagey about revealing her exact location to us... assuming he knew himself at the time."

They were both right. Whatever madness had overtaken me last night when I'd tried to claw at the soil seemed to have dissipated. Perhaps now that I wasn't alone, or was no longer keeping her presence a secret, whatever hold the Daughter had over me was gone. I looked down at the earth, moving past the soil using True Sight, following the roots as they entwined around the luminescent shell, and then to the sleeping form of the Daughter. She was in the exact same position in which I'd found her, which suggested to me that the sleep wasn't natural. It must be some kind of spell or magical state that held her like that.

"Is she okay?" Field asked, realizing what I was doing.

I nodded. "The same as yesterday."

"So, she's just sleeping, or whatever, and fully grown?" Aida asked.

"Yeah," I replied, tearing my vision away from her and refocusing on my friends.

"Basically like Sleeping Beauty?" she smirked.

"A bit like that, yeah," I replied, uncomfortable with the comparison. I suddenly felt annoyed with Aida. Why was she belittling the Daughter? I doubted very much it was her fault that she was in that state—it was most likely due to the cruelty of the other Daughters.

"And when she wakes, Eritopia will be at peace?" Aida pressed.

"They said she would assist in saving Eritopia," Jovi mused. "What do you think's so special about her? I mean, if she's the last remaining hope of Eritopia, she's got to be able to do something that the other Daughters can't."

"Or won't," Field added.

"I'm going to put money on one of you needing to wake her up with a kiss to break the spell," Aida added, arching her eyebrow in my direction.

"Seriously?" I retorted. "Can you not be serious for a second, Aida? This isn't a joke! God knows how long that poor girl's been down there. We know what cruelty the Daughters are capable of—this could have all happened against her will."

Aida frowned at me, and fell silent.

I drew in a breath, instantly regretting chastising her. Why had I snapped at her? I didn't normally get wound up like this. I wondered if it was the Daughter and her effect on me, or just that I was exhausted.

"Let's go and eat," Jovi suggested, easing the tension. "I think we're getting a bit grumpy. The food should still be there."

"Should be," I muttered, turning to face the house. I wasn't actually sure how all that worked, only that it appeared at the same time every day, and presumably vanished at some point as well. I hoped we hadn't missed it. At the mention of food my stomach had started to rumble. It had been a long time since we'd eaten, and I guessed that most of us were suffering from some form of dehydration—just water wasn't enough to replenish the body in that kind of punishing heat.

We made our way toward the back garden. I was last to leave, glancing one last time in the direction of the magnolia tree, knowing I wouldn't be back to visit her tonight. That kind of thing would have to stop—it wasn't safe, because I was still unsure whether or not I could be trusted to be there alone. It might have lessened now that it was out in the open, but the tree still drew me to it.

As I crossed the overgrown lawn, I wondered again about what the last Daughter was capable of. Was she a warrior? The only one with the skill to vanquish Azazel? Or was it all part of some prophecy we knew nothing about, that her waking was a sign of Azazel's rule coming to its end?

Why had the other Daughters looked at me with such interest when we went to visit them?

We needed the Druid to tell us about the last Daughter—the full, uncensored truth this time. We couldn't afford to remain in the dark on Eritopia's matters, not when we were the ones seeing visions and being called to strange trees and discovering women in the earth. We needed to know what was going on, and how much hope of getting home we actually had.

AIDA

After complaining that I was tired during dinner, once I got into bed, sleep completely evaded me. Vita dropped off straight away, and Serena must have been sleeping in the armchair downstairs. We'd asked her if she wanted dinner, but she wasn't hungry and so we'd left her to her night-time vigil over Draven.

I lay back on my pillow, looking up at the ceiling. Vita had left the lamp on, and so I could see the moldy and peeling paintwork. I was sick of this place. The heat, the humidity, the inability to roam anywhere we wanted to, having to stick within the confines of the garden.

Tomorrow I would explore the front garden—at least it would be something new, and I doubted, with the way Draven was, that we'd have Oracle training. I felt bad for the Druid. The Daughters were cruel and vicious. I'd never seen a creature be so calmly methodical in their destruction. To me, their attitude was scarier than the act itself.

I tried not to think about the voices of the shape-shifters that had called to me in the mists—I even hated that they were called that. It was another name for werewolves, but I couldn't imagine two species less alike.

They had known I had werewolf blood in me. They had called me weak, because I couldn't change form. Their taunts had gone on and on, always the same, telling me to shift, telling me I was a sub-species because I couldn't do what was in my nature. That had been bearable. It was when they'd called me to join them that I'd felt like I was going mad. They promised that if I followed them, I could take on my true form—become what I was meant to be, had my blood not been diluted.

I had wanted to follow them so badly. Even if rationally I had known that it was just a ploy, that I would become nothing but dinner, their cries had been so convincing. On the way back through the storm, I had felt something. A jolt in my stomach, like something was moving inside me, something primal and instinctual that wanted *out*.

Enough.

I sat up in bed. I wasn't going to lie here all night dwelling on falsehoods. I would go and see if Serena or Draven needed anything, try to be helpful and get out of my own head.

I got off the bed, careful not to wake Vita. I took the lamp with me, hoping she wouldn't mind. It would only be a problem if she woke up in the night, but she seemed to be in a deep sleep. Creeping out of the room, I jumped as a floorboard creaked underfoot. I paused, making sure it hadn't woken my friend, and then continued. I averted my eyes from the ceiling or the shelves as I hurried down the hallway—this was the spookiest part of the house, and I could practically feel the beady eyes of the preserved animals following me.

Hurrying down the stairs, I held the lamp up high, slightly wary of the shadows and groans of the house. As I reached the main entrance, I saw something move out of the corner of my eye. I spun around, my heart feeling like it had jumped into my mouth.

Idiot.

It was my own reflection, staring back at me with wide eyes from a large, age-spotted mirror. I sighed, irritated at almost giving myself a heart attack. I was about to turn away when I saw a movement in the mirror. I watched open-mouthed as black shapes moved across my bare arms and chest. I crept closer to the mirror. They were runes, flitting across my skin as if there was an invisible hand writing them—a constant stream of symbols and icons appearing and then vanishing again a moment later.

Was the change happening? Had the physical side effects of becoming an Oracle begun?

The lamp trembled in my hand. I looked down at my skin, and saw nothing. It was completely clear, devoid of the runes. When I glanced back up at the mirror, they were still there.

It's just your imagination.

I moved away from the mirror. I was tired, exhausted. My mind was playing tricks on me—having way too much fun in this creepy house. I made my way through the main hallway, heading toward the Druid's room. Once again, I caught sight of myself in the reflection of a glass cabinet. The runes were still there—in my reflection at least. I moved to peer closer, checking it wasn't just the grime on the glass surface that was making me think there were runes appearing.

It wasn't.

As I stared, dumbstruck, my blood running cold, I thought I could see the runes seeping black blood. It reminded me of Draven earlier, when he'd carved them into his skin, but the tar-like substance that appeared to trickle down my arm was nothing like I'd ever seen before…

What is happening to me?

PHOENIX

I'm dreaming.

I was back in the desert. It was cold, the middle of the night, with five different glowing spheres shining down above me like moons. The landscape was deserted, and there was no sandstorm behind me this time.

I knew the Daughters were coming. I wanted to wake up. It was almost like I could see myself from above—the real me yelling at my apparition to get out of there, to run, hide. They were coming.

Sand started to blow ferociously over the dried, cracked earth. I heard the sound of female laughter, low and cruel—

the same way they had laughed at Draven when they took out his eyes.

They appeared suddenly, their limbs golden and toned, their white linen dresses moving provocatively in the breeze and their hair whipping up with the blasts of sand like shining cloaks.

"What do you want?" I asked them, my mouth as dry as the desert beneath me. The red-headed Daughter stepped forward, her golden chains and jewelry jangling as she moved. Her masked face was level with mine—close enough that I could see her violet eyes boring into my soul.

"You must wake her," she whispered. "You must, or all will be lost."

"I—I can't," I stuttered. "I don't know how."

The Daughter shook her head. Her fingers reached upward and she slid them gently down the side of my face. A soft hushing sound escaped her mouth, as if she was reassuring a small child.

"It will take one life to start another," she whispered again. "One life to be sacrificed—yours, Phoenix."

"No, that can't be," I gasped, my whole body tensing for the blow I suspected was about to come. Could they kill me here, in a dream? Did they have that much power, or was this just a nightmare, one I would soon wake up from?

"A gift," the redhead soothed, producing a dagger out of thin air. It was crude, an ancient-looking weapon with the blade chiseled from stone and twine wrapped around the handle. She held it toward me, flat out on her palm.

"Take it," she urged me. "Take it, and cut yourself on the full moon. Let your blood flow onto the soil beneath the magnolia tree so the roots can drink it, and the Last Daughter will be reborn."

Hardly knowing what I was doing, I took the knife from her hand, holding it in my own. The stone was warm, and the edges were sharp despite its appearance.

"Your life will have not been in vain, seer," she told me.

I nodded slowly. Perhaps the Daughters were right. What was one sacrifice to save the lives of so many others? If I could give this one gift to the Last Daughter, perhaps my life would have been worthwhile, short as it was.

"She will thank you for it," the redhead whispered.

"Then it's worth it," I conceded, nodding in agreement as I stared into her violet eyes.

I woke with a start. I could feel perspiration dripping down my back, my hair stuck to the nape of my neck. The dream had been so vivid and real that it took me a while to understand that I was back in the bedroom at the plantation house—safe, with my friends and sister around me.

Shaking my head with annoyance, I realized I'd forgotten to open the bedroom windows. No wonder I was having weird dreams. I was probably delirious with heat. I shifted on the bed, about to rise off it, when something heavy shifted against my leg. I felt around in the darkness, drawing back instantly as I cut my finger on something sharp. Wincing, I felt around for the object again, and my fingers touched twine, and then carved stone. It was a knife. With a shaking hand, I held it up to the moonlight.

The gift from the Daughters.

READY FOR THE NEXT PART OF THE STORY?

Hearts will tangle
Romance will ignite...

Dear Shaddict,

Thank you for reading *A House of Mysteries*.

The next book, **_ASOV 44,_** is called **_A Tangle of Hearts_** and it releases **May 21st, 2017**!

Pre-order your copy now and have it delivered automatically to your reading device on release day — visit: **www.bellaforrest.net**

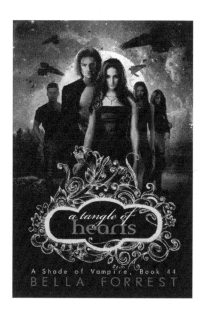

I'll see you again very soon!

Love,
Bella xxx

P.S. Join my VIP email list and I'll send you a personal reminder as soon as I have a new book out. Visit here to sign up: **www.forrestbooks.com** (Your email will be kept 100% private and you can unsubscribe at any time.)

P.P.S. Follow The Shade on Instagram and check out some of the beautiful graphics: @ashadeofvampire

You can also come say hi on Facebook:

www.facebook.com/AShadeOfVampire

And Twitter: @ashadeofvampire

Novak Family Tree

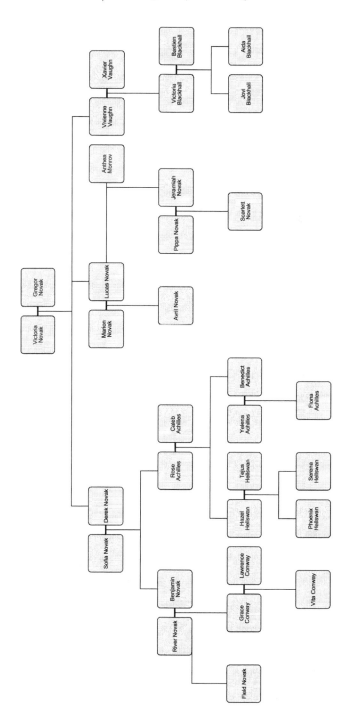

Made in the USA
San Bernardino, CA
24 December 2017